Samuel French Acting Editi

M000281407

Vietgone

by Qui Nguyen

ǁ SAMUEL FRENCH ǁ

ISBN 978-0-573-70647-9

www.concordtheatricals.com
www.concordtheatricals.co.uk

MUSIC AND THIRD PARTY MATERIALS USE NOTE

Licensees are solely responsible for obtaining formal written permission from copyright owners to use copyrighted music and/or other copyrighted third-party materials (e.g., artworks, logos) in the performance of this play and are strongly cautioned to do so. If no such permission is obtained by the licensee, then the licensee must use only original music and materials that the licensee owns and controls. Licensees are solely responsible and liable for clearances of all third-party copyrighted materials, including without limitation music, and shall indemnify the copyright owners of the play(s) and their licensing agent, Concord Theatricals Corp., against any costs, expenses, losses and liabilities arising from the use of such copyrighted third-party materials by licensees. For music, please contact the appropriate music licensing authority in your territory for the rights to any incidental music.

IMPORTANT BILLING AND CREDIT REQUIREMENTS

If you have obtained performance rights to this title, please refer to your licensing agreement for important billing and credit requirements.

VIETGONE was originally commissioned and developed by South Coast Repertory as part of SCR CrossRoads with funding from the Time Warner Foundation. The play received a world premiere co-production by South Coast Repertory (Marc Masterson, Artistic Director; Paula Tomei, Managing Director) on October 4, 2015. The performance was directed by May Adrales, with scenic design by Timothy R. Macabee, costume design by Anthony Tran, lighting design by Jaymi Lee Smith, original music/sound design by Shane Rettig, and projection design by Jared Mezzocchi. The Stage Manager was Kathryn Davies, and the Dramaturg was Andy Knight. The cast was as follows:

ASIAN GUY/AMERICAN GUY/NHAN/KHUE . . . . Jon Hoche

QUANG . . . . Raymond Lee

ASIAN GIRL/AMERICAN GIRL/THU/HUONG/TRANSLATOR/FLOWER GIRL . . . . Samantha Quan

TONG . . . . Maureen Sebastian

PLAYWRIGHT/GIAI/BOBBY/CAPTAIN CHAMBERS/REDNECK BIKER/ HIPPIE DUDE . . . . Paco Tolson

VIETGONE received a world premiere co-production by Manhattan Theatre Club (Lynne Meadow, Artistic Director; Barry Grove, Executive Producer) at Manhattan Theatre Club's Stage I Theatre on October 4, 2016. The performance was directed by May Adrales, with scenic design by Timothy R. Macabee, costume design by Anthony Tran, lighting design by Justin Townsend, original music/sound design by Shane Rettig, and projection design by Jared Mezzocchi. The Stage Manager was Charles M. Turner III, and the Dramaturg was Andy Knight. The cast was as follows:

ASIAN GUY/AMERICAN GUY/NHAN/KHUE . . . . Jon Hoche

QUANG . . . . Raymond Lee

ASIAN GIRL/AMERICAN GIRL/THU/HUONG/TRANSLATOR/FLOWER GIRL . . . . Samantha Quan

TONG . . . . Jenny Ikeda

PLAYWRIGHT/GIAI/BOBBY/CAPTAIN CHAMBERS/REDNECK BIKER/ HIPPIE DUDE . . . . Paco Tolson

VIETGONE was concurrently produced by Oregon Shakespeare Festival on March 30, 2016. The performance was directed by May Adrales, with scenic and costume design by Sara Ryung Clement, lighting design by Seth Reiser, original music/sound design by Shane Rettig, and projection design by Shawn Duan. The Stage Manager was Karl Alphonso, the Dramaturg was Lydia G. Garcia, and the Hip-Hop Coach was Claudia Alick. The cast was as follows:

ASIAN GUY/AMERICAN GUY/NHAN/KHUE .... Will Dao

QUANG .... James Ryen

ASIAN GIRL/AMERICAN GIRL/THU/HUONG/TRANSLATOR/FLOWER
    GIRL .... Amy Kim Waschke

TONG .... Jeena Yi

PLAYWRIGHT/GIAI/BOBBY/CAPTAIN CHAMBERS/REDNECK BIKER/
    HIPPIE DUDE .... Paco Tolson & Moses Villarama

VIETGONE is a recipient of the Edgerton Foundation New American Play Award.

CHARACTERS

QUANG – (M) A helicopter pilot during the Vietnam War. Adventurous, charming, rugged.

TONG – (F) A Vietnamese refugee. Strong-willed, effortlessly sexy, and fiercely independent.

HUONG – (F) Tong's mother. Outspoken, surprisingly flirtatious, unpredictable.

NHAN – (M) Quang's bestfriend. Boisterous, loyal, horny.

BOBBY – (M) American soldier. Naïve, earnest, sweet.

Members of the ensemble may play a variety of supporting characters:

> **AMERICAN GIRL**
> **AMERICAN GUY**
> **ASIAN GIRL**
> **ASIAN GUY**
> **CAPTAIN CHAMBERS**
> **FLOWER GIRL**
> **GIAI**
> **HIPPIE DUDE**
> **NINJAS**
> **PLAYWRIGHT**
> **PROTESTORS**
> **REDNECK BIKER**
> **TRANSLATOR**

NOTES ON MUSIC

Licensees are provided with performance tracks by Shane Rettig for the following songs:

> "Blow 'Em Up"
> "Gonna Start Again"
> "I'll Make it Home"
> "Mary Jane"
> "Lost a Brother"
> "I Don't Give a Shit"

The performance of these songs should be improvisational and performed in the actors' own styles.

The final song, "Mammas Don't Let Your Babies Grow Up To Be Cowboys," by Ed Bruce and Patsy Bruce, is meant to be sung without accompaniment. Rehearsal material is not provided by Samuel French.

ACT I

0.

(A spotlight comes up on an actor playing the **PLAYWRIGHT**.*)*

PLAYWRIGHT. Hi, I'm Playwright Qui Nguyen. I'm here to introduce you to my play *Vietgone*, but first: An official pre-show announcement:

*(***PLAYWRIGHT*** formally reads from a notecard.)*

Welcome to **[insert name of theatre company]**! Woo-hoo!

As the show is about to begin, please make sure cell phones are turned off.

The use of recording devices of any kind is strictly prohibited.

All characters appearing in this work are fictitious. Any resemblance to real persons, living or dead, is purely coincidental.

(That especially goes for any person or persons who could be related to the **PLAYWRIGHT**.*)*

(Specifically his parents.)

(Who this play is absolutely not about.)

(Seriously, if any of you peeps repeat or re-tweet anything you've seen to my folks tonight, you're assholes.)

– And finally, please unwrap any noisy candies now.

To begin, this is a story about a completely made-up man named Quang.

(Lights up on **QUANG**.*)*

9

QUANG. S'up, bitches.

PLAYWRIGHT. ...And a completely not-real woman named Tong.

> *(Lights up on **TONG**.)*

TONG. Whoa, there's alotta white people up in here.

PLAYWRIGHT. And though they are Vietnamese – born and raised there – for the purposes of this tale, it is to be noted that this will be their speaking syntax:

TONG. Yo, what's up, white people?

QUANG. Any of you fly ladies wanna get up on my "Quang Wang"?

PLAYWRIGHT. Which is the opposite of this one:

ASIAN GIRL. Herro! Prease to meeting you! I so Asian!

ASIAN GUY. Fly Lice! Fly Lice! Who rikey eating fly lice?

PLAYWRIGHT. And on the occasion – when it occurs – that an American character should appear, they will sound something like this:

AMERICAN GUY. Yee-haw! Get'er done! Cheeseburger, waffle fries, cholesterol!

PLAYWRIGHT. Spouting American nonsense which sounds very American but yet incredibly confusing for anyone not natively from here.

AMERICAN GIRL. NASCAR, botox, frickles!

PLAYWRIGHT. This is a story about two people –

Both from Vietnam –

Both thirty years of age –

Both survivors of a conflict that's been raging in some form or fashion their entire lives –

However though it will be a story that will often hop back and forth in time – in and around said conflict – this is not a story about war – it's a story about falling in love. And it all takes place in the year of 1975.

> *[Projection: July 1975]*

> *[Projection: Arkansas]*

(Lights up on **QUANG** *riding a motorcycle. His bestfriend,* **NHAN,** *is holding onto him for dear life.)*

And right now, the completely made-up Quang Nguyen is with his best friend Nhan taking a road trip from Fort Chaffee, Arkansas all the way to Camp Pendleton, California.

[Projection: Vietgone]

(A beat drops...)

[Music Cue 01: "Blow 'Em Up"]

*(***QUANG** *is rhyming to himself for fun as they blaze down the highway.)*

QUANG.
    YELLA MUTHAFUCKAH ON A MOTORCYCLE
    RIDING SO FAST LIKE HE'S SUICIDAL
    DRIVING 'CROSS AMERICA TO CATCH A FLIGHT TO
    HIS HOME CITY SO HE CAN GO HOMICIDAL

    IN SAIGON
    CITY IN VIETNAM
    SHOT UP BY THE VIET CONG
    THEY STOLE MY PEEPS' FREEDOM
    SO I'M COMING TO KILL THEM
    CALL ME THEIR ARCH-VILLAIN
    CAN'T STOP ME I'M WILLIN'
    TO DIE FOR THIS VISION

    OF A VIETNAM THAT'S FREE
    FROM THOSE EVIL VC
    YOU CAN'T STOP ME
    I'M LIKE A PISSED OFF BRUCE LEE
    WITH A HI-YA, A KICK, AND A KUNG FU GRIP
    WE'LL COME OUT SWINGING, WE DON'T GIVE NO SHITS

NHAN. Dude –

QUANG.
    SO IMMA BLOW'EM UP, BLOW'EM UP, BLOW'EM ALL UP!

NHAN. Hey!

QUANG.

> SHOOT'EM UP, SHOOT'EM UP, SHOOT THEM ALL UP!

NHAN. STOP!

QUANG.

> WE TWO BAD MUHFUCKERS HEADED TO WAR
> AND WHEN WE GET BACK HOME, WE'RE GONNA KILL THEM
> ALL!

NHAN. STOP STOP STOP STOP STOP!!

QUANG. What in the / hell, man?

NHAN. Will you PLEASE stop rhyming and driving at the same time? You're going to get us killed!

QUANG. Homie. I'm just enjoying the ride, bro. It's awesome.

NHAN. It's the antithesis of awesome.

QUANG. We're like American cowboys. John Wayne and shit.

NHAN. John Wayne did not sit bitch behind his best buddy on a rusted out death bike.

QUANG. This is not a rusted out death bike.

> This is a rusted out awesome bike.
>
> Ain't that right, girl?

NHAN. Well, I wanna see you say that when this hunk of junk strands us in the middle of "Nowhere, America."

QUANG. She's not going to strand us.

> You're not going to strand us. Are you, baby?

NHAN. Can you care a little less about this piece of crap motorcycle and a little bit more about your bro – your bro who doesn't want to die right now!

QUANG. Homie, why are you freaking out? I thought you were excited about my plan.

NHAN. Your plan is to murder us?

QUANG. The plan is drive to California. Catch a plane to Guam. Then once we're in Guam, we just hop a boat back to Vietnam. That's a solid ass plan.

NHAN. We couldn't have taken a plane or train to California? Can't we wait to afford a ride that has – like – a roof?

QUANG. Look, do you want me to bring you back to that refugee camp? We've only been on the road for like thirty minutes – it ain't that far away.

NHAN. No. Don't be mad.

(They ride quietly for a spell.)

So how'd she take it?

QUANG. Who?

NHAN. That girl you were seeing.

QUANG. I wasn't seeing no girl.

NHAN. Dude –

QUANG. Homie, I'm married. I have a wife and kids who are still in Vietnam. It doesn't matter what anyone thinks – especially just some random girl I met at some camp.

NHAN. Yeah, but –

QUANG. We don't belong here. We belong there.

There, we're heroes. We're sons. We're men.

There, we count for something.

Here, however, we ain't shit.

NHAN. I know, but –

QUANG. Bottom line, we're going home.

NHAN. Right. We're going home.

1.

[Projection: Four Months Earlier]

[Projection: Saigon, South Vietnam]

(Lights up on a pretty Vietnamese woman, TONG [30], sitting at the edge of a bed. Lying in the bed is a man named GIAI [30] weeping inconsolably.)

(TONG just sits waiting and listening in hopes that he'll calm down soon.)

(He doesn't.)

TONG. Okay, can you stop crying now? Please.

> *(GIAI tries to pull it together.)*
>
> *(He stares deeply into TONG's eyes.)*
>
> *(And then breaks back down in tears.)*

GIAI. I just don't understand why you won't marry me.

TONG. Well, you crying about it like you are is really making me want to change my mind.

GIAI. It is?

TONG. No.

GIAI. Don't you love me?

TONG. Um. Sure I do?

GIAI. YOU DON'T LOVE ME?!

TONG. It has nothing to do with that.

GIAI. Then what does it have to do with?

TONG. It's just the thought – the idea of marrying you, being your bride, committing myself to you, it makes me want to...well...kill myself.

GIAI. OH GOD!

TONG. But it's not personal.

GIAI. It's Bic, isn't it? You still having feelings for Bic.

TONG. It's not Bic. Bic's a dick.

GIAI. But you have feelings for him?

TONG. Would it make a difference if I did?

GIAI. It'd at least be a reason. A real reason other than just "no."

TONG. Okay, fine, I love Bic.

GIAI. YOU DO?! WHY WOULD YOU STILL LOVE HIM?! HE'S A DOUCHEBAG!

TONG. I don't!

GIAI. But you just said –

TONG. Giai. Listen to me. I'm sorry I don't have a reason for saying "no" other than it just being no. Maybe I'm just a bitch. There's mounting evidence that indeed may be the case.

GIAI. Don't say that. You're wonderful. I love you.

TONG. Well, maybe you're also crazy...

GIAI. Crazy in love.

TONG. Or just plain crazy.

GIAI. I can give you a life. I have money. I have a house. A motorbike. A nice motorbike. It's Japanese. Don't you want a guy with a nice Japanese motorbike?

TONG. Though that's tempting...

GIAI. I can take care of you.

TONG. That's sorta the thing. I don't want anyone taking care of me.

GIAI. But you're a woman.

TONG. I'm aware of my gender.

GIAI. Do you not want a family?

TONG. Sure I do.

GIAI. But you're thirty.

TONG. I'm also aware of my age.

GIAI. If you don't have children soon, your ovaries will dry up. You'll have dry ovaries. Do you want to be like one of "those women"?

TONG. A woman with dry ovaries?

GIAI. A woman without children.

TONG. Oh god, that would be horrible!

GIAI. Right?

TONG. I was being sarcastic. I actually enjoy my —

GIAI. Listen to me. I love you.

> (GIAI *starts to whimper.*)

I love you more than anything in this world. Ever since I met you, you have changed my life.

> (GIAI *can't hold it together.*)

You're everything to me. All I want is to make you happy, to give you the life you deserve, to free you from any pains that you have —

> (*He's full-on crying now.*)

Please please please marry me.

TONG. Giai —

GIAI. PLEASE!

TONG. Fine. I'll think about it, okay? Just stop crying. And begging. Please.

GIAI. You'll really think about it?

TONG. Yes.

GIAI. Really?

TONG. Yes. Really.

GIAI. Okay. OKAY! I will take that. I will take it! I will turn that maybe into a yes. I love you! / You just watch, I will convince you of what I already know. You and I are soulmates, Tong Thi Tran. I love you!

TONG. Yeah, okay. Thank you for that. That was really... something.

> (GIAI *leans in and starts passionately kissing* TONG...*except* TONG *isn't really passionately kissing him back. Or at all.*)
>
> (*She finally stops him.*)

GIAI. I love you.

TONG. I heard you the first time.

GIAI. You are like a flower blossoming in the field of my soul and —

TONG. Hey, do you maybe just wanna do it?

GIAI. What?

TONG. Yeah, all this love talk is really making me horny.

> *(She straddles him.)*

GIAI. I knew you LOVED ME...

> *(GIAI starts crying again. From happiness.)*

TONG. Just shut / up!

> *(Cut to...)*

> **[Projection: Saigon military station]**

> *(Soldier boy QUANG [early 30s] waits for someone to arrive at the gates. His boy NHAN runs up to him with a great idea:)*

NHAN. Yo, bro, great idea!

QUANG. I don't wanna know.

NHAN. We should get hookers!

QUANG. We should not get hookers.

NHAN. Okay, not "we." Me.

QUANG. Don't get a hooker.

NHAN. Come on! The Americans get hookers all the time! Don't you wanna be American?

QUANG. No.

NHAN. Yo, man, why not?

QUANG. STD's for one.

NHAN. I'll wear a condom.

QUANG. Crabs don't give a crap about no condom, bro.

NHAN. I'll shave my shit afterwards.

QUANG. You're also broke. I'm pretty sure a guiding principle to getting a hooker to hook is the ability to throw down cash for that ass. You got cash?

NHAN. Yeah, about that... I was actually wondering if I could borrow –

QUANG. No.

NHAN. Oh, come on.

QUANG. No.

NHAN. Please.

QUANG. No.

NHAN. You're like the worst friend of all friends.

QUANG. Because I actually give a damn about you not getting syph, that makes me a bad friend?

NHAN. Quang –

QUANG. No.

NHAN. Look, homie…

There's something you should know.

There's something I ain't ever told you before.

QUANG. What's that?

NHAN. Don't judge me, but I still got my v-card.

QUANG. What?

NHAN. I'm a…virgin.

I know it's surprising. It's just – I just want to know what it's like to be with a woman before I die. To know what it's like to be that close to someone. Any moment right now could be our last. The VC is literally right outside these –

QUANG. The pimply chick from *Nha Trang*, the tall girl with the black teeth from *Bao Loc* –

NHAN. You knew about them?

QUANG. Yeah. So go on with your virginity monologue.

NHAN. Neither of them were particularly good lays.

QUANG. A lay is a lay, my friend. You're no virgin.

NHAN. I'm a born-again virgin.

QUANG. NO.

NHAN. You know what, Quang Nguyen? If you wanted a hooker, I'd get you hooker. A clean hooker. Because I'm an awesome friend and awesome friends get friends HOOKERS!

(NHAN *storms out. As he does,* THU *enters.*)

THU. Hi Nhan.

NHAN. Thu!

(NHAN *hugs her.*)

It's been so long! How are you? You look great by the way. Can I borrow some money?

QUANG. NO!

NHAN. Your husband sucks.

(NHAN *storms out, angry.*)

THU. Hey.

QUANG. Hey. You / look beautiful.

THU. You're as handsome as ever.

(*They share a laugh. It's small, but genuine.*)

QUANG. It's been –

THU. A long time.

QUANG. Can I kiss you?

THU. Of course you can.

QUANG. Okay. Here we go. Kiss coming atcha. Watch out.

(*They kiss.*)

THU. I'm sorry I couldn't come sooner.

QUANG. We just got re-stationed here a week ago. One week is pretty damn impressive.

(*They kiss again. But this time with a lot more meaning.*)

So where's Trang and Quyan?

THU. I didn't bring them.

QUANG. THU!

THU. They're with my parents.

QUANG. But you said –

THU. I know what I said, but –

QUANG. I haven't seen them in months.

THU. I just didn't think it was smart –

QUANG. It's been almost a year.

THU. I know.

QUANG. Thu, this is really messed up.

I don't even have a picture of them right now.

THU. What happened to the ones I sent you?

QUANG. They were on the console of my Huey when it got shot down.

THU. WHAT?!

QUANG. I didn't tell you about that, did I?

THU. You were shot down?

QUANG. Just barely.

THU. How barely?

QUANG. It's classified?

THU. QUANG! How could you not tell me about that? You could've died!

QUANG. Hey, don't flip this on me. I'm mad at you. You don't get to be mad at me until I'm done being mad at you. You didn't bring the kids!

I even got Trang a thing. It's a teething giraffe.

THU. She's four.

QUANG. Four-year-olds don't teethe?

THU. It's fine, I'll just give it to Quyen.

QUANG. I got him this knife.

THU. You got a two-year-old a knife?

QUANG. It's a cute knife?

THU. Quang, do you not know anything about children?

QUANG. Well, no. It's not like I've really had the chance.

THU. I'm sorry.

QUANG. Why didn't you bring them?

THU. There's rumors.

QUANG. What rumors?

THU. About the VC. About how close they are.

QUANG. They're always close.

THU. But this sounds like –

QUANG. Like what? Like they're in our backyard? Of course they are. That's where they live. They're like communist gophers. Doesn't mean they're gonna win

though. Have you seen what we got? The Americans
got us packing all kinds of crazy heat.

THU. I'm glad you're so confident, but –

QUANG. Hey, you do remember what I do, right? Look at
me. I'm a pilot. A badass pilot. If the shit ever really
went down, I'd just haul us the hell out of here.

THU. Is that really a plan?

QUANG. Yes.

THU. Quang –

QUANG. Listen to me, if the Viet Cong ever breech Saigon,
I will fly us away. I promise.

> *(They kiss. But with meaning this time.)*
>
> *[Sound Cue: Explosion]*
>
> *(Cut to…)*
>
> *[Projection: Three weeks later…]*
>
> *(Sirens are going off as Irving Berlin's "White
> Christmas"* plays over loud speakers. In the
> distance we hear gun fire and chaos.)*

NHAN. What in the hell?!

QUANG. Operation Frequent Wind.

America's pulling out.

Saigon's falling.

NHAN. Oh man, we gotta get outta here!

QUANG. Okay, grab your gear. We gotta hit the sky.

---

*A license to produce *Vietgone* does not include a performance license
for "White Christmas." The publisher and author suggest that the
licensee contact ASCAP or BMI to ascertain the music publisher and
contact such music publisher to license or acquire permission for
performance of the song. If a license or permission is unattainable for
"White Christmas," the licensee may not use the song in *Vietgone* but may
create an original composition in a similar style or use a song in the
public domain. For further information, please see Music Use Note on
page 3.

NHAN. There's a gun-copter commandeered down by Hanger 18.

QUANG. Good.

NHAN. The USS Midway is just off the peninsula of *Vung Tau.* We can get there in like thirty.

QUANG. We gotta do a touchdown in *Soc Trang* first.

NHAN. That's the opposite direction.

QUANG. My family's there.

NHAN. Man, there's something you should know about this copter.

QUANG. Tell me in flight. We need to book, motherfucker! Let's go! LET'S GO!

> (QUANG *and* NHAN *bolt.*)
>
> (*As they do, we see other anonymous Vietnamese refugees frantically zip across the stage with make-shift suitcases in hopes of finding a way to escape Saigon.*)
>
> (*Moments later,* QUANG *runs up to the helicopter and peers in. He immediately turns back to* NHAN.)

Who in the hell are all these people?

Get them out!

NHAN. Dude, I can't.

QUANG. There's no room for anyone else.

NHAN. I know, but –

QUANG. I need to be able to fit three more people. Get them out.

NHAN. Dude, there's kids in there.

QUANG. Not my kids.

NHAN. Look, man, *Soc Trang* is two hundred kilometers from here. Thu and your kids are safe. Viet Cong ain't gonna roll that far south now that they have Saigon. These peeps on the other hand are plant food if we leave them here.

QUANG. I don't mean to be heartless –

NHAN. We can't just bail on them. Who knows what those commie bastards will do? For all we know, they'll just bury all these people. Is that what you want?

Listen, the USS Midway is only a half-hour shot from here. We drop off all these peeps and I will go with you to *Soc Trang* to grab your family. I promise. Don't let these kids die.

QUANG. Okay. OKAY. Let's do this. But we move fast – we move efficient. We drop off, re-fuel, and go. Got me?

NHAN. Gotcha!

QUANG. Ladies and Gentlemen, I am Captain Quang Nguyen of the 225th Helicopter Squadron of the Republic of Vietnam's Air Force. I'll be flying you all to freedom. Buckle up!

> *(Cut to…)*

> ***[Projection: Fort Chaffee, Arkansas]***

> **(TONG** *is standing by a bare bunk-bed with her suitcase in hand.)*

> *(Music plays:)*

> ***[Music Cue 02: "Gonna Start Again"]***

TONG.

> IT'S APRIL 29, 1975
> WE SOUTH VIETS GO FLEEING TO SAVE OUR LIVES
> A MASS IMMIGRATION, PEEPS DEALT DEVASTATION
> HUMILIATION IN THE FACE OF COMPLETE ANNIHILATION

> OF A DREAM SEIZED BY THE VC
> KILLING ANY HOPES OF A SOUTH VIET DEMOCRACY
> BUT WON WITH GUNS AND THE MURDER OF SONS
> THOSE ON THE RUN HAVE LOST EVERYONE

> IRONICALLY WE'RE THE ONES THEY CALL THE LUCKY ONES
> BUT CAN WE MAKE A NEW LIFE NOW THAT OUR OLD LIVES ARE DONE?
> AMERICA TRIES TO HELP US ALL START OVER
> BY PUTTING US IN CAMPS IN THE MIDDLE OF NOWHERE

TONG.

> THEY GOT CAMP PENDLETON IN CALIFORNIA
> EGLIN AIR FORCE BASE IN THE MIDDLE OF FLORIDA
> THEY GOT CAMP INDIANTOWN IN PENNSYLVANIA
> AND WHERE I LAND, SOME SPOT CALLED ARKANSAS
>
> GONNA START AGAIN – NOW THAT SAIGON'S GONE
> GONNA START AGAIN – STEEL MY SOUL, MAKE IT STRONG
> GONNA START AGAIN – NOT A DIME TO MY NAME
> GONNA START AGAIN – GET MY HEART PAST THIS PAIN
>
> GONNA START AGAIN – GOODBYE TO MY OLD LIFE
> GONNA START AGAIN – MAKE WHAT'S LEFT OF ME RIGHT
> GONNA START AGAIN – IN THIS NEW COUNTRY
> AND IT ALL STARTS HERE – IN FORT CHAFFEE
>
> WE GET TO AMERICA BY ANY DESPERATE MEANS
> 'CAUSE THEY SAY THEY'LL TAKE THE POOR AND THE WEAK
> BUT DOES THAT GO FOR REFUGEES THAT LOOK LIKE ME
> PEEPS REMINDING THEM OF THEIR ENEMY?
>
> NOW IN AN ARMY BASE COVERED WITH SOLDIERS
> BEATEN UP BUNKERS NOT MADE FOR COMFORT
> VIETS PILED ON TOP OF ONE ANOTHER,
> CRAMMED TOGETHER – WE'RE JUST ANOTHER NUMBER
>
> ALL WE GOT NOW IS WHAT'S ON OUR BACK
> THE MOST BASIC THINGS IN LIFE NOW WE LACK
> THE ODDS AGAINST US ARE COMPLETELY STACKED
> TRYING TO FORGET OUR OLD LIVES NOW COMPLETELY
> CRACKED
>
> AND HERE I TELL ME I CAN'T BE HURT AGAIN
> SINCE EVERYONE I KNOW IS EITHER LOST OR DEAD
> CONVINCING MYSELF THE END IS NOT THE END
> BUT A BED TO BIRTH A NEW DIRECTION
>
> GONNA START AGAIN – NOW THAT SAIGON'S GONE
> GONNA START AGAIN – STEEL MY SOUL, MAKE IT STRONG
> GONNA START AGAIN – NOT A DIME TO MY NAME
> GONNA START AGAIN – GET MY HEART PAST THIS PAIN
>
> GONNA START AGAIN – GOODBYE TO MY OLD LIFE
> GONNA START AGAIN – MAKE WHAT'S LEFT OF ME RIGHT

GONNA START AGAIN – IN THIS NEW COUNTRY
AND IT ALL STARTS HERE – IN FORT CHAFFEE

SO ANGRILY – I LOOK INSIDE OF ME
I STAND DEFIANTLY – THOUGH MENTALLY MY MIND'S A
CATASTROPHE
I PREP TO FIGHT THIS SITCH I NOW EXIST IN – KEEP
PERSISTING
PUSH MY HEART AND MY SOUL BEYOND REASON
YOU THINK IMMA FAIL, CHECK YOUR FACTS, SON
I'M THE QUEEN OF THE HILL, BITCH, KEEP RESPECTIN'
THE BADDEST BITCH IN THE CAMP, I'M TONG TRAN, MAN
UNDERSTAND – IF YA WANNA STEP TO ME I'LL KNOCK YOU
ON YOUR ASS

GONNA START AGAIN – NOW THAT SAIGON'S GONE
GONNA START AGAIN – STEEL MY SOUL, MAKE IT STRONG
GONNA START AGAIN – NOT A DIME TO MY NAME
GONNA START AGAIN – GET MY HEART PAST THIS PAIN

> *(An American soldier,* **BOBBY***, enters and spots
> her.)*

> *(She doesn't notice him as he looks at her. He can't
> believe how beautiful she is. He checks his breath,
> straightens out his shirt, and fumbles with his hair
> before getting his nerves up to approach.)*

TONG.

GONNA START AGAIN – GOODBYE TO MY OLD LIFE
GONNA START AGAIN – MAKE WHAT'S LEFT OF ME RIGHT
GONNA START AGAIN – IN THIS NEW COUNTRY
AND IT ALL STARTS HERE – IN FORT CHAFFEE

> *(***BOBBY*** pokes her on her shoulder as she sings.)*

OH MY GOD!

> *(The music abruptly stops.)*

BOBBY. Sorry am me. Me am so sorry. Me am work here.

TONG. Uh… What are you saying?

BOBBY. Sorry. Me Vietnamese not good.

TONG. That's fair. My English is also pretty damn atrocious.

BOBBY. Me am checking list?

> (**BOBBY** *shows her his clipboard.*)

This you?

TONG. Yep, that's me.

BOBBY. This you bed?

TONG. Looks like it.

BOBBY. Check!

Good bed. Hard. Good lie down.

TONG. Is it now?

BOBBY. To sleeping! Good bed to sleeping. See?

Ah, so nice.

> (**BOBBY** *lies down in her bed to show her what he's trying to explain.*)

TONG. I see.

BOBBY. What me doing?

Me am so sorry.

> (**TONG** *is tickled seeing how nervous* **BOBBY** *is.*)

TONG. It's fine.

BOBBY. Me am so rude. Me am name Bobby.

TONG. Tong.

BOBBY. Tong.

TONG. Bobby.

BOBBY. Tong needing anything in camp, ask Bobby. Bobby is Tong Friend. Number one friend!

TONG. I'll keep that in mind.

BOBBY. Meeting you nice it is, Tong.

TONG. Meeting you is very nice as well, Bobby.

> (**TONG**'s *mom,* **HUONG**, *walks in and sees the two of them giving each other eyeballs.*)

HUONG. Oh god, what are you doing? Are you actually coming on to a American soldier? How pedestrian is that?

TONG. Shut up, Mom.

HUONG. Hi.

BOBBY. Nice to meeting you, old lady.

> *(He bows to her. She's annoyed.)*

HUONG. His Vietnamese sucks.

TONG. Mom.

BOBBY. Pretty you are, old lady. Like daughter is mother.

HUONG. Thanks, dumb American!

BOBBY. No problem, old lady!

HUONG. Why'd you leave me?

TONG. I didn't leave you. I told you I was going to find where we were staying while you were picking out clothes.

HUONG. I could have gotten lost.

TONG. But you didn't.

HUONG. Why are you still standing here?

BOBBY. Check?

HUONG. What?

BOBBY. Check face.

HUONG. Check what?

BOBBY. Check brain? No. Not brain. Me lost word. Um, it is –

HUONG. I. DON'T. UNDERSTAND. YOU!

TONG. Your name, Mom. He's checking your name off his list.

> *(TONG goes and looks over BOBBY's list over his shoulder. He clearly likes being so close to her.)*

Yes. That's her. That's my mom.

BOBBY. Check.

TONG. Can you hand me those sheets?

HUONG. You can go away now.

BOBBY. Welcome to Fort Chaffee!

Goodbye, Tong.

TONG. Bye, Bobby.

HUONG. BYE!

> (**BOBBY** *exits.*)

TONG. So did you find anything?

HUONG. This.

> (**HUONG** *shows* **TONG** *a tacky worn out t-shirt with the state of Arkansas on it.*)

TONG. That's...cute?

HUONG. No one gave me time to pack.

TONG. Yes, how inconsiderate of me.

HUONG. All the clothes here are terrible.

TONG. I found some nice things.

HUONG. This room is terrible.

TONG. I know, Mom.

HUONG. This place is terrible.

TONG. I know, Mom.

HUONG. Are we actually going to sleep in bunk beds? Bunk beds? When did we sprout penises and join the army?

TONG. Do you see any other options?

HUONG. I thought we'd have our own rooms at least.

TONG. It's a refugee camp, Mom. It's not a hotel.

HUONG. I know it's not a hotel. I just thought – well, it's America. I thought everything would be super nice here in America. That's sorta what they advertise.

TONG. You know, we don't have to share the same bunks. Maybe you'd be happier sharing space with someone your own age.

HUONG. No way. There might be crazy people here.

TONG. Why is it only crazy people are the ones worried about potentially running into other crazy people?

HUONG. What's that supposed to mean?

TONG. Nothing, Mom.

HUONG. We're in a foreign country – we have no home, no money – we can't even speak the language.

TONG. I took English in school.

HUONG. Okay, fine, one of us can speak an elementary level of English – congratulations – being able to say "Hi, hello, that is a library," will make all the difference. But this is a very serious situation. I'm not letting my only living daughter out of my sight –

TONG. Aw. Are you actually worried about me?

HUONG. Well, you're also the one who dragged me here so you're absolutely responsible in taking care of me.

TONG. And there it is.

HUONG. I'm taking the bottom!

TONG. Mom, I didn't "drag you here." We were days away from being overrun by the Viet Cong, my job at the embassy offered me two tickets to America, I gave you one of those tickets – to, you know, SAVE YOU.

HUONG. You saved me?

TONG. Yes. I saved you. This is the act of being saved.

HUONG. I'm old. Do you know how old I am?

TONG. Still young enough to annoy the fuck out of me.

HUONG. I'm OLD! I mean – don't get me wrong I'm still quite attractive for my age, but I'm old – in my twilight years – the golden years – the last chapter – one foot in the grave –

TONG. Your point?

HUONG. You can't save me from the inevitable.

TONG. Oh God, you're going to talk about dying again.

HUONG. Your father – my darling Muu – passed away ten years ago and is waiting for me to join him on the other side.
I miss you, darling. Yes, I love you. But I have to make sure our dummy kids can take care of themselves before I can join you.

TONG. Are you serious?

HUONG. I'm at death's door!

TONG. One. You are not at death's door. Or death's driveway. And the fact that you're now here in America where bombs aren't falling down on you means you aren't even in death's zip code anymore. So stop it. And Two. Dad was fifteen years older than you and – even then – he died from pneumonia, not old age. You are very far from either your golden or your twilight years. Since we've been here, how many Americans have already mistaken you for my older sister? They think you're forty.

HUONG. Well, that's because white people age faster than Vietnamese. They look really old really fast. That boy you were just talking to was probably just ten.

TONG. He wasn't ten.

HUONG. Bottom line, dear, you should have brought your brother here.

TONG. Trust me, Mom, that was the original plan. But he said –

(Spotlight on KHUE.)

KHUE. There's no way.

TONG. It's a trip to America, Khue. AMERICA!

KHUE. I'm not going.

TONG. It's free.

KHUE. I have to stay.

TONG. Because of Pham?

KHUE. Yes, because of Pham.

TONG. You'll find a new bang piece, little brother. She's just a girlfriend.

KHUE. She's not just "a girlfriend."

TONG. Are you married? Do you have kids that I don't know about?

KHUE. No.

TONG. Then she's just a girl, Khue. One girl. I'm your sister.

KHUE. Pham's the love of my life.

TONG. Really?

KHUE. Really.

TONG. That's your answer? "The love of my life."

Fucking fuck, Khue, the communists are going be rolling into our streets any day now with the mind to make dead all of us who aren't waving red flags and you're going to stick around to get riddled with bullets because Pham is some sort of fairy-tale idea of love you've concocted in your brain?

KHUE. She's not a fairy tale. She's real. Our love is real. And if you don't have an extra seat for her to come with me, then I'm staying here by her side.

TONG. That's stupid.

KHUE. I'm not going.

TONG. No, you're going to fucking go! Come here.

> (TONG *tries to pick up* KHUE *and drag him out of the room.*)

KHUE. What are you doing?

TONG. I'm making you come with me.

KHUE. This is ridiculous, Tong. Let go of me.

TONG. No, Khue, I'm not going to leave you here. I'm not I'm not I'm not! You're going to go, do you hear me? You're going to come with me to America and we're going to become American and eat greasy foods and listen to Elvis!

KHUE. Tong!

TONG. No, I'm not going to let you die. I'm not going to let you die here. I can't. I CAN'T. That would destroy me. It would absolutely destroy me.

KHUE. I know. And that's how I feel about Pham.

I know you don't know what this feels like. I know you have no idea, especially ever since Bic left you.

But this is real. She's it for me. I'm not leaving her. Not ever. Even if it means…

TONG. What am I supposed to do?

KHUE. Bring Mom.

TONG. Mom? Right? Like she'd ever come with me.

KHUE. She loves you.

TONG. No, she loves you. You're her golden boy – her prince. I, on the other hand, am her thirty-year-old burden who looks like she's never going to get married because she's never met "the love of her life."

KHUE. I'll make sure she goes.

TONG. How do I say goodbye to you, little brother? We've been a team our whole lives. You're my best friend.

KHUE. Then don't.

TONG. Don't what?

KHUE. Don't say it. I'll see you again.

TONG. Promise?

KHUE. Promise.

> *(They hug.)*
>
> *(Cut to...)*
>
> **[Projection: USS Midway]**
>
> *(Lights come up on* QUANG, NHAN, CAPTAIN CHAMBERS, *and a* TRANSLATOR.*)*

CAPTAIN CHAMBERS. Captain Nguyen!

TRANSLATOR. Yo, you Captain Nguyen?

QUANG. I am.

CAPTAIN CHAMBERS. Me am pirate king hi-ho Midway. Here yellow banana ventriloquist.

TRANSLATOR. "Greetings, I'm Captain Chambers of the USS Midway and this fine motherfucker right here is my translator".

QUANG. Nice to meet you, sir. Thank you for taking all of us in.

CAPTAIN CHAMBERS. Whoop whoop, fist bump. Mozzarella sticks, tator tot, french fry.

TRANSLATOR. "You should be very proud. You saved many lives today. Congratulations."

CAPTAIN CHAMBERS. Shit-eating grin?

TRANSLATOR. "You must be very relieved to be alive."

QUANG. Not really, sir. My family is still over there. I really should get back to my copter. And quick.

CAPTAIN CHAMBERS. Mysterious science, what what?

TRANSLATOR. "What?"

QUANG. I need to get to my helicopter. I need to go back.

CAPTAIN CHAMBERS. Poopy pants.

TRANSLATOR. "Oh man, this is awkward."

QUANG. What's awkward?

CAPTAIN CHAMBERS. Splish splash taking a bath.

TRANSLATOR. Really? That's messed up.

CAPTAIN CHAMBERS. Splish splash taking a bath. Tell tell.

QUANG. What are you guys talking about? I don't really have time for this. I should –

TRANSLATOR. Sorry, bro. You don't have a helicopter.

QUANG. I just airlifted three dozen civilians here in it, what do you mean I "don't have a helicopter"?

CAPTAIN CHAMBERS. Splish splash.

TRANSLATOR. "We pushed it off the carrier to make room for incoming planes. Too many copters were coming at one time. We needed space so we pushed it off into the sea."

QUANG. What? NO!

CAPTAIN CHAMBERS. Shit-ass. USA! USA!

TRANSLATOR. "I'm so sorry about your loss, but there is no going back. You're coming to America now."

QUANG. I don't want to go to America!

CAPTAIN CHAMBERS. Shit-ass.

TRANSLATOR. I'm sorry.

QUANG. You're sorry?
   SORRY!
   No. That's not – NO! You have to let me go back. You have to let me go back! Please!

CAPTAIN CHAMBERS. Fuck a duck, yella fella. Fuck a duck.

TRANSLATOR. "So sorry, bro. There's just no way. Have a nice ride."

(NHAN carefully approaches.)

NHAN. So, um, America. Yay! That's the dream, right?

(NHAN puts his hand up for a high five.)

That's a setup for a high five. It's an American thing – they do this when they celebrate stuff.

You're supposed to give it up!

As in…slap it.

Or… I'll just…do it myself.

(NHAN high fives himself.)

Look, man. I'm sorry.

If it weren't for me, we would have got your family. –

Look, man, if it makes you feel any better, you can punch me if you want. I understand –

(QUANG suddenly punches him.)

Did that help?

QUANG. Nope. Not even remotely.

> *(Music begins playing. QUANG takes the stage solo, trying to gather back up his strength.)*

[Music Cue 03: "I'll Make it Home"]

I'M BROKEN, BUT UNBREAKABLE
DEFEATED, YET UNDEFEATABLE
UNSTOPPABLE 'GAINST THE IMPOSSIBLE
I'LL GET HOME HOWEVER IMPLAUSIBLE
JUST WATCH ME – UNFAZEABLE
MY TENACITY'S UNWAVERABLE
MY LOVE FOR MY KIDS AND SAIGON –
INDESTRUCTIBLE

MY COUNTRY'S NOW FALLEN, A NEW MISSION'S NOW CALLING,
AMERICA'S WITHDRAWN, MY CALL'S TO FINALLY COME HOME AND
TRADE IN MY GUN FOR MY SON, MY SOLDIER'S LIFE'S NOW DONE
GOT 99 PROBLEMS, BUT THE WAR AIN'T ONE

I'LL HOLD MY KIDS IN MY ARMS AGAIN – DO YOU *HEAR ME?*
NOTHING STOPPING ME – EASILY – DO YOU FEEL ME?
MY FAMILY'S GONNA BE WITH ME – DO YOU SEE ME?
GONNA MAKE IT BACK TO MY HOME – EVEN IF IT KILLS
ME…

WHERE THE HELL AM I GOING
I DON'T KNOW BUT I'M KNOWING
HOWEVER IMPOSSIBLE THIS IS
I'LL MAKE IT BACK TO MY HOMELAND

HOME
I'LL MAKE IT HOME

WHERE THE HELL AM I GOING
I DON'T KNOW BUT I'M KNOWING
HOWEVER IMPOSSIBLE THIS IS
I'LL MAKE IT BACK TO MY HOMELAND

HOME
I'LL MAKE IT HOME

> *(Lights up on* **TONG** *in Fort Chaffee.)*

TONG.

I LEFT MY BRO ALL ALONE IN A HOME THAT'S ALL BLOWN
UP
LOST ALL THE THINGS THAT I'VE KNOWN – MY HEART'S
HAD TO GROW UP
FASTER THAN PLANNED AS MY SOUL'S NOW ALL TORN UP
SAY BYE TO MY LIFE – NOT RIGHT – IT'S ALL MESSED UP.

THIS AGONY INSIDE OF ME AIN'T PROVIDING ME ANY TIME
TO THINK
ABOUT ANYTHING BEYOND THE SITCH WE'RE NOW LIVING
GOTTA GO HARD, GOTTA BE TOUGH
GOTTA MOVE FORWARD TOWARDS A NEW DAWN, A NEW
DREAM, A NEW HOPE

FUCK THIS SITCH – I'M A WARRIOR, BITCH
THE WORLD KEEPS HITTING – I DON'T GIVE NO SHITS
JUST WATCH ME NOW, BRO – I'LL MAKE YOU PROUD
THEY CAN PUNCH ME – STAB ME – BUT I WON'T GO DOWN

WHERE THE HELL AM I GOING
I DON'T KNOW BUT I'M KNOWING

HOWEVER IMPOSSIBLE THIS IS
I'LL MAKE THIS PLACE MY NEW HOMELAND

HOME
I'LL MAKE IT HOME

WHERE THE HELL AM I GOING
I DON'T KNOW BUT I'M KNOWING
HOWEVER IMPOSSIBLE THIS IS
I'LL MAKE THIS PLACE MY NEW HOMELAND

HOME
I'LL MAKE IT HOME

> *(As they sing, the world around* **QUANG** *transforms from the USS Midway into walls outside of Fort Chaffee where* **PROTESTERS** *stand with signs like "Gook go home!")*

GREETED BY HATE SIGNS, NOT HIGH FIVES

QUANG.

– THEY DISLIKE US

TONG.

THIS IS WHERE WE'LL BUILD A NEW LIFE

QUANG.

– THEY DESPISE US

TONG.

A NEW HOME GROWN FROM AN ARMY BASE

QUANG.

IN A COUNTY NOT KNOWN FOR LOVE FOR PEEPS WITH A YELLOW FACE

TONG.

A PLACE WHERE OUR KIDS WILL THINK OF US WITH DISGRACE

QUANG.

AFTER ALL THE YEARS I FOUGHT, IT WAS ALL JUST A WASTE.

TONG.

NOW THE PAIN IN MY BRAIN KEEPS ME UP ALL NIGHT

QUANG.

DREAMING 'BOUT MY FAMILY WORRYING IF THEY'RE ALRIGHT

TONG.

REGRETTING A LIFE NOW FULL OF "COULDA BEEN'S"

QUANG.

AS WE STRIVE TO BE MORE THAN SECOND CLASS CITIZENS

TONG.

WHAT'S COMING NEXT IS ALL FEELING GRIM –

QUANG.

AS WE STARE AT ALL THE SHIT WE'RE NOW STANDING IN.

TONG.

WHERE THE HELL AM I GOING?

QUANG.

I DON'T KNOW BUT I'M KNOWING

TONG.

HOWEVER IMPOSSIBLE THIS IS –

QUANG.

I'LL MAKE IT BACK TO MY HOMELAND

TONG.

HOME

I'LL MAKE IT HOME.

BOTH

WHERE THE HELL AM I GOING

I DON'T KNOW BUT I'M KNOWING

HOWEVER IMPOSSIBLE THIS IS

I'LL MAKE THIS PLACE MY NEW HOMELAND

HOME

I'LL MAKE IT HOME

2.

[Projection: Oklahoma City, Oklahoma]

(QUANG and NHAN are riding down the highway.)

(As they ride, a REDNECK BIKER rolls up beside them on the highway. On his bike is a large Confederate flag flapping in the wind.)

(He sees QUANG and NHAN. NHAN smiles and waves.)

(This for some odd reason enrages the REDNECK BIKER, and he tries to run them off the road.)

(There's a bump and run fight between the two bikes as they slam into each other and try to knock each other down.)

(Finally, NHAN pulls off his own helmet and begins beating the biker. Eventually the biker loses control and spills out, while QUANG and NHAN ride off into the distance.)

NHAN. What in the hell was that about?

QUANG. What? You ain't never studied any American history before?

NHAN. Why would I do that?

QUANG. They helped us fight a war. You don't think learning a bit about them would be a good idea?

NHAN. I'll start next week.

QUANG. Americans aren't huge fans of peeps like you and me.

NHAN. Bullshit. Why would they send so many troops over if they didn't like us?

QUANG. Listen, man, I spent eighteen months here in '68 learning how to fly down in Lackland Air Force Base. They barely like each other. Look how the white ones treat the black ones here and they're all from the same country.

NHAN. That is nutbags.

QUANG. This is why we need to get home. North and South Vietnam may be at war, but at least we're not fighting each other over something as stupid as the way we look.

NHAN. Word.

QUANG. Word.

> *[Projection: One Month Earlier]*
>
> *[Projection: Fort Chaffee, Arkansas]*
>
> (HUONG *and* TONG *are in a cafeteria.*)

HUONG. I hate this place.

TONG. I know, Mom.

HUONG. Do you see what they feed us? Meat. Just plates of meat. And vegetables that have been so deep fried they only taste like grease and salt.

TONG. I know, Mom.

HUONG. It's horrible here.

TONG. And you think being back in Vietnam right now where the commies are probably evicting people out of their homes and stealing all their life savings for the state is what? Amazing?

HUONG. But it's our home. Where your brother is. And his beautiful girlfriend Pham. I love Pham!

TONG. I know.

HUONG. Oh God, I hope she's okay.

TONG. Khue's smart. I'm sure he's fine. They probably headed south.

HUONG. I hope so.

TONG. I miss him too.

HUONG. I WANT TO GO BACK!

TONG. I wish that were possible.

    If I could send you back, Mom, I would. I so would.

HUONG. That's not funny.

TONG. Mom, you need to give this place a chance. Unlike home, Americans actually figured out how to

do a democracy. Hell, they made it up. If you earn
something here, no one takes it away from you.

HUONG. I guess that's good.

TONG. That's great.

So can you please give it a chance?

HUONG. How?

TONG. I signed us up for a thing.

HUONG. What thing?

TONG. Well, for you, some English classes and then for
me –

HUONG. I'M NOT LEARNING ENGLISH!

TONG. Mom, we live in America now. Americans speak
English. We need to be able to speak with them.

HUONG. Why can't they learn Vietnamese?

TONG. Yes, because that is a rational plan. That's totally
what's going to happen. We'll just cross our arms and
wait for all the Americans to learn Vietnamese. How
long do you think that's gonna take?

HUONG. I've been on this earth over fifty years. I've learned
everything I need to learn. I've raised eight kids. I've
survived two husbands. Wars. I'm not going to waste my
time learning a language that I'm never going to speak
because I know we're going to go back to Vietnam.

TONG. How?

HUONG. I don't know yet. But it's going to happen.

TONG. Have fun with that plan.

HUONG. Have fun taking your English class alone.

TONG. I didn't sign up for English, I signed up for
something else.

HUONG. What? A cooking class? So you can make...meat
and deep-fried potatoes?

TONG. I signed up for a foster family.

HUONG. You have a family. Me.

TONG. Yeah. And you wonder why I'd want to leave?

HUONG. You're thirty. People don't adopt thirty-year-olds.

TONG. It's not that kind of foster family. It's a program where I live in an American home for six months and they help me get a job, find my own place, assimilate to the culture.

HUONG. That sounds terrible.

TONG. I think it's kinda cool.

HUONG. You're just going to go be American? Is that it? Go live with an American family?

TONG. Yep.

HUONG. And what am I supposed to do?

TONG. I thought you were going back to Vietnam so who cares, right?

HUONG. In the meantime...

TONG. I don't know, Mom. Hang out here in this camp. Make some friends. Write some letters. If you're not going to work with me to make this a better experience then you're on your own.

HUONG. So who's this family?

TONG. I don't know yet. I'm on a waitlist.

HUONG. Well maybe I'll sign up too.

TONG. Good luck finding the American family that speaks only Vietnamese

(*The American soldier,* **BOBBY**, *approaches.*)

BOBBY. Tong! Hi. Me. Bobby.

HUONG. It's him again.

You know he wants to fuck you, right?

TONG. MOM!

HUONG. He doesn't know what I'm saying. Look at him. He's stupid.

(**BOBBY** *smiles and innocently nods.*)

(**TONG** *looks in her English dictionary to find the right word to greet* **BOBBY**.)

TONG. "How-Dee." Bobby.

BOBBY. Git'er done, lil Lassie! Yee haw. "Howdy."

TONG. HOE-Dee?

BOBBY. Howdy.

TONG. HOW-Dee.

BOBBY. Howdy.

TONG. How-DEE?

BOBBY. Howdy.

TONG. Howdy.

HUONG. Goddamn, English is a terrible language.

BOBBY. Bacon Cheeseburger McDonald's?

TONG. I'm not following.

BOBBY. Bacon. Cheeseburger. McDonald's.

TONG. Am I...hungry?

BOBBY. Nixon!

TONG. Oh yeah, I am hungry. Thank god for this amazing meal before us.

> (TONG *points to her terrible meal.*)

BOBBY. Better I can get you.

TONG. Yeah?

BOBBY. Yum yum.

HUONG. Is he going to offer you his meat now?

TONG. Mom.

BOBBY. Town good food. Bring you can I.

TONG. I would love to...

> (HUONG *suddenly grabs her chest, has a "heart attack," and falls down dead.* TONG *doesn't even react.*)

...But not today, okay? I should stick with my mom.

BOBBY. Oh. Okay.

HUONG. Yes, white boy, you're going to have to go through Mama Bear if you want to get in this pot of honey!

TONG. Don't listen to her. I mean – it's not like you can understand her, can you?

BOBBY. Mommy of yours is very pretty old lady.

HUONG. Seems like a keeper.

TONG. Check with me next week, okay?

BOBBY. Okay.

HUONG. You can't be serious.

TONG. None of your business, Mom. None of your business.

>   (**TONG** *smiles as she bites into her food.*)

Holy crap, this shit is terrible!

>   (*Cut to...*)

>   (**NHAN** *and* **QUANG** *entering the camp.*)

NHAN. Dude. America looks like a prison.

QUANG. It's a refugee camp. Of course it looks like a prison.

NHAN. Hold up. Except prisons don't got that!
Look.
Ladies.

QUANG. Yes, Nhan. Immigrants come in girl as well.

NHAN. What did you just say?

QUANG. Girl?

NHAN. No. Before that.

QUANG. Immigrants?

NHAN. Fuck, man. That's what we are now, isn't it?
Immigrants.

QUANG. That's only if we stay. But, yes, we're technically immigrants.

NHAN. Maaan, I don't wanna be an immigrant.
Immigrants talk funny. People are mean to immigrants.
When the Chinese come to Vietnam, no one's nice to
them. That's what we are now. We're the Chinese.
FUCK!
I don't want to be Chinese.

QUANG. Don't worry. It's not like Americans can tell the difference anyhow.

NHAN. This is terrible.

QUANG. You weren't very nice to the Chinese, were you?

NHAN. Fuck them. I hate the Chinese – fucking commie bastards!

QUANG. Yeah. Karma's a bitch.

Look, I'm gonna go find us some food. You go find out where we get blankets and shit for our bunks.

NHAN. Will do.

> (QUANG and NHAN split up.)
>
> (As NHAN leaves...)

(To himself.) Man, I don't want anyone to think I'm fucking Chinese.

> (Cut to...)
>
> (As QUANG enters the cafeteria with tray in hand, HUONG spots him.)
>
> (She likes what she sees.)
>
> (She grabs something off her plate and throws it at him to get his attention.)

HUONG. Hello.

QUANG. Hi.

HUONG. You're new.

QUANG. Yep.

HUONG. And shapely.

QUANG. What?

HUONG. Would you like to join me? My younger sister just left.

> (She grabs him and pulls him to her table.)

QUANG. Sure. I guess.

> (She grabs a water pitcher...)

HUONG. Would you like something to –

> (...And dumps it on his shirt.)

Oh, sorry. Clumsy me. Let me help you with that.

> (She grabs a napkin and dabs at his chest as she makes sexy eyes at him.)

QUANG. How old are you?

HUONG. Age-appropriate.

QUANG. Cool.

I'm married.

HUONG. What?

QUANG. Yeah, married. Married years old. That's me. Super married.

HUONG. Oh. I'm sorry, I –

QUANG. It's cool. Whatever.

(And I think I can dry my own chest, thank you.)

HUONG. Sorry. Can't blame a single thirty-nine-year-old woman for trying.

QUANG. I'm flattered.

HUONG. So where is she?

QUANG. Where's who?

HUONG. Your wife.

QUANG. Oh. Um. Still in Vietnam.

HUONG. Oh, I'm so sorry. I thought –

QUANG. I know.

(They sit quietly for a beat.)

HUONG. This is super awkward. I should just leave you to your lunch.

QUANG. It's okay. It's cool. Please stay.

HUONG. Are you sure?

QUANG. I insist.

(QUANG begins eating his food as HUONG watches him.)

HUONG. I know what it's like.

QUANG. You know what what's like?

HUONG. Losing a spouse.

QUANG. I haven't lost a spouse –

HUONG. I had two. Both dead. Not my fault.

QUANG. Oh, I'm sorry.

HUONG. It was a long time ago. My first husband died from a heart attack and my second died from pneumonia while we were living in a leaf hut in Saigon.

QUANG. You lived in a leaf hut?

HUONG. When the communists came into *Mo Duc*, they either ran out or executed anyone who owned property. To save ourselves, we escaped to Saigon. But we had no money, no home – that is until my oldest daughter Tong came up with the plan to make a house out of tin sheets and banana leaves. We lived there for almost three years until my husband got sick and died.

QUANG. Your daughter sounds resourceful.

HUONG. She's a bitch. I mean I love her, but she's crazy.

QUANG. That seems harsh.

HUONG. I don't mean to be. It's just – she doesn't think like I do. For one, she actually likes it here.

QUANG. Fort Chaffee?

HUONG. America.

QUANG. She likes America?

HUONG. Yes.

QUANG. Yeah, that is crazy.
First chance I get, I'm getting the hell out of here and going home.

HUONG. Oh yeah?

QUANG. Yeah.

HUONG. Well if you can figure that out, then can I come with you?

QUANG. Sure.

HUONG. I'm Huong by the way.

QUANG. Quang.

HUONG. Nice to meet you, Quang.

(They shake hands.)

So firm.

3.

[Projection: Amarillo, Texas]

(QUANG *and* NHAN *are at picnic table.*)

NHAN. What is this?

QUANG. It's called a burrito. You eat it.

NHAN. It's like a fat spring roll.

QUANG. Just eat it.

(NHAN *takes a bite.*)

NHAN. Goddamn.

QUANG. Right?

NHAN. This is American food?

QUANG. It's Mexican.

NHAN. Yo, whatever it is, it is delicious. Why are we trying
to go back?

QUANG. We're not too far from where I went to flight
school. I got to fly a TH-55 there.

NHAN. Those little bug-looking copters?

QUANG. That's the one. Fun little machines. Not very fast
though. seventy-eight knots at most. There's cars that
book faster than that. But I wanna see a car jump over
a goddamn tree, right?

NHAN. See! America has all the cool shit. Don't you wanna
stay where all the cool shit is?
Look, you know I'm your bro – but there's something I
need to say to you –

QUANG. Shhh!

(A HIPPIE DUDE *and* FLOWER GIRL *approach*
NHAN *and* QUANG *as they eat.*)

HIPPIE DUDE. Peace love, my peace love!

FLOWER GIRL. Flower power.

(QUANG *goes immediately cold.*)

QUANG. S'up.

HIPPIE DUDE. Vietnamese?

NHAN. That's right.

FLOWER GIRL. Chinese?

NHAN. NO, NOT CHINESE!

FLOWER GIRL. Japanese!

NHAN. You were right the first time, we're –

FLOWER GIRL. KOREAN!

NHAN. VIET. NA. MESE! We're Vietnamese Vietnamese Vietnamese!

FLOWER GIRL. Filipino?

QUANG. Your English is for shit, dude.
    Cheeseburger, baseball, discrimination.

HIPPIE DUDE. Right on, daddio, you talk good English like cat cool. Meow.

QUANG. Yep.

HIPPIE DUDE. So you two dudes be Vietnamese?

QUANG. We are.

FLOWER GIRL. Cool that, yo.

HIPPIE DUDE. That be cool.

QUANG. Cool.

HIPPIE DUDE. Can we give you two cat cools some love?

NHAN. What?

HIPPIE DUDE. Love, man, you want love?

QUANG. Whoa. I don't think we're into that.

NHAN. I'll take some love from that hippie girl.

HIPPIE DUDE. Not that love, cat cool.
    We mean puff love.

QUANG. Puff?

FLOWER GIRL. Burn, blaze, chill cool with the Buddha bro.

HIPPIE DUDE. Doobie, brotha. Doobie.

        (**HIPPIE DUDE** *pulls out a joint.*)

NHAN. Is that what I think it is?

QUANG. Yep.

NHAN. Man, I've always wanted to try –

HIPPIE DUDE. So what say you, cool breeze?

QUANG. Yeah, bro. We'll party. Let's party.

HIPPIE DUDE. Right on!

*(The **HIPPIE DUDE** lights it up as music begins to play.)*

[Music Cue 04: "Mary Jane"]

QUANG.

MARY JANE WASH AWAY
ALL THIS PAIN THAT'S IN MY BRAIN
TAKE MY SOUL TO A PLACE THAT'S CALM
LEMME FORGET I LOST MY BABY'S MOM

LEMME SMILE – LET IT NOT BE FAKE
PUT ME IN A NEW MENTAL STATE
WIPE AWAY THIS SAD ATTITUDE
EVEN IF THIS JOY IS JUST DRUG INDUCED

I DON'T WANNA THINK ABOUT WHERE I AM
A SOLDIER LOST IN SOME FOREIGN LAND
I DON'T WANNA THINK ABOUT THE SHIT I MISSED
MY WIFE, MY COUNTRY, MY TWO YOUNG KIDS

THIS IS BULLSHIT
I DON'T WANT THIS
I WANT TO GO HOME
BUT IT'S ALL GONE
JUST HELP ME
SOMEBODY
PLEASE FREE ME
OF THIS MISERY

SO DO YOUR TRICK SWEET CANNABIS
ERASE AWAY MY MENTAL SADNESS
HERE WE GO, BURN IT UP
FILL MY LUNGS I DON'T GIVE A FUCK

JUST KILL MY THOUGHTS, MAKE ME NUMB
DESTROY THE MEMORIES OF WHAT WENT WRONG
WRAP YOUR SMOKE AROUND MY THROAT
CHOKE ME OUT SO I WON'T KNOW

QUANG.

THAT I MISS MY KIDS, I MISS MY WIFE
I MISS VIETNAM, IS THIS MY LIFE?
I'M ALIVE BUT SO ALONE
I CAN'T BELIEVE I LOST MY HOME

THIS IS BULLSHIT
I DON'T WANT THIS
I WANT TO GO HOME
BUT IT'S ALL GONE
JUST HELP ME
SOMEBODY
PLEASE FREE ME
OF THIS MISERY

GOD ARE YOU UP THERE WATCHING ME
RAGING HERE WITH THIS HOSTILITY
PLEASE – DON'T LET THIS BE – MY REALITY
THAT THIS QUEST IS JUST A QUEST – IN FUTILITY

I JUST WANNA SEE MY BOY GROW UP TO BE A MAN
HEAR MY DAUGHTER CALL ME DAD
HOLD THEM BOTH AND SING THEM SONGS
DON'T TELL ME – THESE DREAMS ARE GONE

DESTROY THESE DOUBTS INSIDE MY MIND
SLAY MY FEARS, LEMME KNOW I'M FINE
OR GO AHEAD AND JUST BURY ME
I DON'T WANT A LIFE WITHOUT THEM NEXT TO ME

THIS IS BULLSHIT
I DON'T WANT THIS
I WANT TO GO HOME
BUT IT'S ALL GONE
JUST HELP ME
SOMEBODY
PLEASE FREE ME
OF THIS MISERY

THIS IS BULLSHIT
I DON'T WANT THIS
I WANT TO GO HOME
BUT IT'S ALL GONE

JUST HELP ME
SOMEBODY
PLEASE FREE ME
OF THIS MISERY

> *(Cut to...)*

> **[Projection: Fort Chaffee]**

> (**TONG** *is busy carrying laundry.*)

> (**GIAI** *appears.*)

GIAI. Hey babe. So have you thought it over yet?

TONG. Giai?

GIAI. Miss me?

> (**GIAI** *starts to cry from happiness.*)

TONG. Oh my God!

> (**TONG** *drops the clothes and runs up and hugs him tight.*)

I didn't know you were here.

GIAI. I followed you. Because I love you.

TONG. You followed me?

GIAI. As your plane was taking off, I grabbed onto the wheel and climbed into the cargo bay.

TONG. How's that possible?

GIAI. And now I'm here. With you. Together. Forever.

TONG. Giai, I can't believe how happy I am to see you.

GIAI. So do you have an answer for me?

TONG. What?

GIAI. Will you marry me?

TONG. Giai.

My answer is...yes.

GIAI. What?

TONG. Yes. Yes, I'll marry you.

GIAI. I knew it. I knew I could convince you! I knew you loved me!

TONG. Okay, Tiger, don't get too excited.

GIAI. You're going to be my wife, how can I not be excited about that! This is the best day EVER!

(*He starts to cry again.*)

(*TONG notices something on GIAI's shirt.*)

TONG. What's that on your shirt?

GIAI. What?

(*It's a red mark that keeps growing.*)

Hm. That's weird.

(**GIAI** *unbuttons his shirt that's quickly getting soaked in red.*)

(*As he opens his shirt, there are bullet holes riddled across his chest.*)

Oh fuck. I think I'm dead.

(*Suddenly the world turns very spooky and menacing.*)

Just like your brother and your father and now me... We're all dead. Dead dead dead.

(**KHUE** *enters the room. He's covered in blood and gunshot wounds.*)

KHUE. Sis? Why'd you go?

TONG. Khue?

KHUE. Why'd you leave me?

All alone?

(**KHUE** *begins bleeding from his mouth, eyes, and ears.*)

(**KHUE** *immediately falls dead.*)

(**TONG** *screams.*)

[Image Projection: Shots of dead Vietnamese flood the stage.]

(*Cut to...*)

(**TONG** *asleep in bed, having a nightmare.*)

(**QUANG** *walks in and spots her lying there.*)

QUANG. Ahem. Excuse me. Hello?

(**TONG** *is asleep.*)

(**QUANG** *doesn't know what to do. Should he poke her? No, she might freak out if a stranger were touching her in her sleep.*)

(*He instead tries clapping very loudly.*)

HELLO!

(*Nothing.*)

(*He tries to clap again.*)

HELLO, HELLo!

(*Nada.*)

(*He begins stomping up and down, clapping, and in general being very loud.*)

HELLO HELLO HELLO HELLO HELLO –

TONG. SHUT UP!

QUANG. Oh, sorry, did I wake you?

TONG. Who are you? What do you want?

QUANG. My name's Quang. I'm a friend of your mom's.

TONG. You know my mother?

QUANG. Yep. Crazy old lady who thinks she looks thirty-five?

TONG. That's her.

QUANG. Yep, I know her.

TONG. And she knows you?

QUANG. Yes.

TONG. What do you want with her?

QUANG. I'm helping her with something.

TONG. What something?

QUANG. A project.

TONG. What project?

QUANG. Okay, detective, enough with the third degree. We both have a mutual desire.

TONG. EW.

QUANG. No, I don't mean we have a mutual desire of each other. We both have a desire to go back to the motherland.

TONG. Ew.

QUANG. Did you just "ew" our motherland?

TONG. No. Yes. Sorta. Okay, I did.

QUANG. She was right about you.

TONG. What was she right about?

> (**TONG** *gets out of bed and finally makes eye contact with* **QUANG**. *It rattles both of them.*)

QUANG. That you are…very…fine.

> (*He's surprised he just ended his sentence the way he did…*)

TONG. My mom said I'm "very fine"?

> (*…But now he goes right into flirt mode.*)

QUANG. Yes. She said "I have a daughter and she is muhfucking fine." Yo, your mom has a potty mouth.

TONG. Are you hitting on me?

QUANG. No. Yes. Sorta. I guess I am.

TONG. …

QUANG. Okay, whatever, tell your mom I came by and that she should find me at dinner.

And sorry about waking you up…it looked like you were having a bad dream anyhow.

I can't sleep worth a damn here either. Too many ghosts up there, right?

TONG. Right.

QUANG. See you round.

> (**QUANG** *starts to leave…*)

TONG. Hold up.

QUANG. What?

TONG. I'm not really in the mood to be alone right now.

QUANG. Should I go find your mom?

TONG. No, I have a better idea. Come here. I want to see something.

> (QUANG *cautiously approaches.*)
>
> (*Once he gets close enough,* TONG *grabs him and rips off his shirt.*)

QUANG. Whoa, what are you doing?

> (TONG *examines* QUANG*'s body.*)

TONG. That'll work.

QUANG. What will work?

TONG. Okay. Let's do it.

QUANG. Do what exactly?

TONG. Do IT. Intercourse. Copulate. Play hide-the-hot-dog.

QUANG. Are you serious?

> (TONG *takes off her dress.*)

TONG. Or would you prefer we keep awkwardly talking? What do you say?

QUANG. Well... I...say –

> (QUANG *grabs her and they begin furiously making out as lights go to black.*)

End of Act I

ACT II

4.

[Projection: Amarillo, Texas]

(QUANG *and* **HIPPIE DUDE** *are still chilling as* **NHAN** *and* **FLOWER GIRL** *are making out.)*

HIPPIE DUDE. This is a cool night, right? A cool night for a cool breeze.

QUANG. Man, I don't know if it's the dope, but I'm understanding you totally clear right now.

HIPPIE DUDE. Right on, man. Right on.

QUANG. And, homie, sorry about your girlfriend.

HIPPIE DUDE. That's not my girlfriend, man.

QUANG. Well, that's good. 'Cause she's definitely working on some international relations right now with her tongue.

(QUANG puts his hand up for a high five.)

HIPPIE DUDE. Naw, bro, that girl's my wife.

QUANG. Say what?

HIPPIE DUDE. Free love, my man. Free love.

(HIPPIE DUDE puts his hand up for a high five.)

QUANG. You American fools are fucking weird.

(HIPPIE DUDE high fives himself.)

HIPPIE DUDE. Alright. Hey my Asian brotha from another mother, can I tell you something?

QUANG. Yeah, what's that?

HIPPIE DUDE. This has been on my mind and in my heart ever since we first saw you yesterday. Maybe even before that.

QUANG. Spit it out.

HIPPIE DUDE. From the bottom of my heart – the bottom of my soul – I just wanna say – from me, from us, from America – we are really sorry.

QUANG. For what?

HIPPIE DUDE. For what we did to your country.

QUANG. Um, there's nothing to apologize for –

HIPPIE DUDE. No, man, there is. Look, I get it. Make love, not war.

QUANG. Is that right?

HIPPIE DUDE. I just wanted to let you know, it was an equally unpopular war here. All us cats that didn't go over, we were working to make sure the war ended as soon as possible.
You're welcome.

QUANG. You're an idiot.

HIPPIE DUDE. What?

QUANG. I mean – no offense – maybe you're not, maybe it's just the weed talking, but right now you sound dumb as a motherfucker. You have no idea what you're talking about.

HIPPIE DUDE. I watched the news, man.

QUANG. So what?

HIPPIE DUDE. I protested.

QUANG. Great.

HIPPIE DUDE. Hey man, I lost a brother over there. I know what's up.

QUANG. I'm sorry. I really am. But that still doesn't make you an expert on what I've actually gone through.

(A beat drops…)

[Music Cue 05: "Lost a Brother"]

QUANG.

NO MOTHERFUCKER ACTUALLY WANTS TO HAVE WAR –
BUT YA NEVER HAD WAR KNOCKING ON YOUR FRONT DOOR
NEVER HAD IT BLOWING UP YOUR STREETS
GOT NO IDEA WHAT DYING EVEN TRULY MEANS
NEVER SEEN IT KILLIN' THOSE YOU LOVE
NEVER BEEN DRENCHED IN YOUR OWN BROTHA'S BLOOD
NEVER HAD SOMEONE TRY TO SHOOT YA DEAD
SON, WAR'S MORE THAN JUST SOME THEORY IN YOUR HEAD

YOU LOST A BROTHA
I LOST MY FAMILY
YOU LOST A BROTHA
I LOST MY WHOLE COUNTRY
YOU LOST A BROTHA
I LOST MY WIFE AND KIDS
YOU LOST A BROTHA
MOTHERFUCKER, I LOST EVERYTHING I HAD

SO TIE YOUR RIBBONS AROUND YOUR OLD OAK TREES
BUT SAVE YOUR SORRIES AND IGNORANT APOLOGIES
DON'T PUT WORDS IN THE MOUTHS OF THOSE WHO DIED
CAUSE IT WAS THROUGH THEIR SACRIFICE THAT I HAVE MY
LIFE
YO, I'M HERE ALIVE IN HONOR OF THEIR MEMORY
'CAUSE IF IT WEREN'T FOR THEM THERE WOULD BE NO ME
YOU MIGHT BE SMART – GREAT – YOU READ SOME NEWS
BUT YOU DON'T KNOW SHIT ABOUT THE SHIT WE ALL
WENT THRU

YOU LOST A BROTHA
I LOST MY FAMILY
YOU LOST A BROTHA
I LOST MY WHOLE COUNTRY
YOU LOST A BROTHA
I LOST MY WIFE AND KIDS
YOU LOST A BROTHA
MOTHERFUCKER, I LOST EVERYTHING I HAD

QUANG.

> IT MUST BE NICE FIGHTING FIGHTS WITH JUST WORDS AND
> SIGNS
> BUT YOU'RE NOT THE ONE NEXT TO ME ON THE FRONT
> LINE
> SO WHEN YA TELL ME YA THINK IT'S ALL JUST BULLSHIT
> YOU'RE TELLING ME THAT MY FAMILY WASN'T WORTH IT
> EVERY STORY, HOWEVER GORY, HAS ANOTHER SIDE
> 'CAUSE YOU DISAGREE DON'T MEAN YOUR OPINION'S
> RIGHT
> SO FUCK YOU, FUCK YOUR WORDS, AND WHAT YOU SAID
> YOUR SORRY TELLS ME THAT YOU'D RATHER SEE MY KIDS
> DEAD
>
> YOU LOST A BROTHA
> I LOST MY FAMILY
> YOU LOST A BROTHA
> I LOST MY WHOLE COUNTRY
> YOU LOST A BROTHA
> I LOST MY WIFE AND KIDS
> YOU LOST A BROTHA
> MOTHERFUCKER, I LOST EVERYTHING I HAD

> *(Cut to...)*

> ### *[Projection: Fort Chaffee, Arkansas]*

Holy God. Did that really just happen?

TONG. Yeah, that was awesome... I mean...it was okay.

QUANG. Oh, hey. Should I go?

TONG. No. Yes. Maybe. I don't know.

QUANG. I feel like I should apologize or something?

TONG. For what?

QUANG. For making love to you?

TONG. "Making love"?

> Do you even know my last name?

QUANG. It's...

TONG. Do you even remember my first name?

QUANG. Thi?

TONG. Tong.

QUANG. I was actually spelling it out. First letter is T. The rest is ONG.

TONG. What we did was not make love. There was no "love" between these sheets. There was some stress, a bit of rage, and a shitload of frustration, but love had nothing to do with what we just did.

QUANG. You're…nice.

TONG. What?

QUANG. I mean I get it – you've been through some shit. We all have. You don't have to be so glower about it.

TONG. Excuse me, person I don't know at all, are you really sitting here criticizing my personality?

QUANG. I'm just saying –

TONG. That I'm a bitch?

Sure. And proud, baby.

Deal with it.

QUANG. You know what?

TONG. What?

QUANG. You're right.

TONG. I'm what?

QUANG. You're right. I was out of line.

TONG. That's it?

QUANG. That's what?

TONG. You're just going to back down? Just like that?

QUANG. Why would I argue?

TONG. Cause you're a Vietnamese man and Vietnamese men are all fucking assholes.

QUANG. We're not all fucking assholes. Yes, some of us are, BUT some of us – I would like to think – are very good upstanding people who not only think of others, but are also –

TONG. Is that a wedding ring?

I take it by your silence that is indeed a wedding ring. You're an asshole.

QUANG. Damn, man. You're right. I am an asshole.

TONG. It's okay. I'm a bitch. Thus why we get along.

QUANG. That must be it.

TONG. So how'd you and my mom meet anyhow?

QUANG. She hit on me.

TONG. Ew.

QUANG. Tell me about it.

TONG. My mom is so gross.

QUANG. Naw, she's cool, man. She just wants to go home to take care of your baby brother.

TONG. You mean my baby brother who's twenty-two?

QUANG. She made it sound like he was still a toddler.

TONG. Well, he is the youngest after all which means he'll always be in diapers to her.

QUANG. I have two kids myself.

TONG. Yeah?

QUANG. Yep. The oldest is four and the youngest is two.

TONG. What are they like?

QUANG. Um, well, the oldest is four. And the youngest is two.

And they're both cute.

TONG. Wow, you don't know jack about your kids.

QUANG. Well, to be fair, my oldest kid is four years old and I've been in the military for eight. So you do the math.

TONG. Your kids aren't yours?

QUANG. No, they're mine.

I just haven't seen them very much. You know there being a war and all, I've probably spent a total of two months with them their whole entire lives.

TONG. Wow.

QUANG. So I really owe it to them to get back. To be there.

TONG. Even if it means going back in a box?

QUANG. What?

TONG. I'm sorry. I shouldn't say that. That's terrible of me.

QUANG. No, it's okay. Everyone I talk to, I can tell it's in the back of their head.

TONG. But it is a possibility, right? I mean, who knows what's even happening over there? It's not like we can call someone up for an update. For all we know, everyone in South Vietnam is locked up in their death camps. You know, the very opposite of "all good in the hood."

QUANG. It doesn't matter. I gotta go back.

TONG. Do me a favor. Don't die, alright? I mean, not like I care, but you're a pretty good lay so that would be a waste.

QUANG. Thanks. You're not so bad yourself.

(They begin kissing some more. HUONG enters.)

HUONG. What. The. Fuck?

TONG. Hey Mom. I met your buddy. He's awesome.

HUONG. WHAT THE FUCK?!

QUANG. Oh man, she's mad.

HUONG. You're engaged!

TONG. Well, he's married.

QUANG. Don't throw me under the bus with you.

TONG. I'm just saying – I'm not the guiltiest one here.

HUONG. So you two you, you – you –

TONG. We fucked, Mom.

HUONG. Oh god.

TONG. What? You're always worried that I won't meet someone. Well, I met someone. In my pants.

HUONG. You weren't supposed to meet him.

QUANG. What's wrong with "him"?

HUONG. Get the fuck out.

QUANG. So do you not want to talk about how we're getting to Camp Pendleton?

HUONG. Get out!

QUANG. Okay. Thanks for the – uh – sex.

TONG. Anytime.

> (QUANG *and* TONG *high five. He exits.*)

HUONG. Do you have to be a whore?

TONG. I'm not a whore, Mom. I was horny. And sad. Plus mad. More sad and mad than anything else, but that helped.

Tremendously.

He seems like a decent fella.

HUONG. He just cheated on his wife with you.

TONG. Well, yeah. But besides that, he seems alright.

For a military dude, he's not all alpha asshole at all. He's actually pretty soft.

HUONG. Are you actually saying something nice about a man?

TONG. Yes. I like men. Just not most of them.

HUONG. You cannot like this guy.

TONG. I don't.

HUONG. Seriously, you cannot like him.

TONG. I. Don't.

HUONG. He's married. He's going back to Vietnam. And he's my ride. Stay away from him. Do you understand me? Stay. Away.

TONG. It was a one time thing. I promise I'll stay away.

HUONG. Thank you.

> (HUONG *storms off.*)

TONG. Goddammit. Now I *really* wanna fuck him.

> (*Cut to…*)
>
> (*Movement [live montage] sequence: To a song in the style of a sexy '70s R&B song.* TONG *and* QUANG *keep running into each other and*

---

*A license to produce *Vietgone* does not include a performance license for any '70s R&B songs. The licensee may create an original composition in a similar style or use a song in the public domain. For further information, please see Music Use Note on page 3.

*immediately start "getting it on" through different '80s inspired sequences [***TONG*** at a pottery wheel as **QUANG** wraps her arms around her à la Ghost, **BOBBY** holding a boombox to steal her attention but thwarted as **QUANG** holds up an even bigger boombox à la Say Anything, meeting up at the "Fort Chaffee" social which breaks into a* Dirty Dancing*-style group dance number, etc.)*

*(Throughout, **HUONG** and **NHAN** find different funny ways to interrupt the lovers.)*

(With each hook up, the following days of the week click forward in projection:)

Sunday

Monday

Tuesday

Wednesday

Thursday

Friday

Saturday

*(It culminates with **TONG** and **QUANG** finally together, slow-dancing. In this final moment, **HUONG** once again catches them…but seeing that their affections for each other are real, she leaves them alone to continue their romantic duet.)*

5.

[Projection: Albuquerque, New Mexico]

(**QUANG** and **NHAN** *riding through the desert.*)

NHAN. Holy shit, man, look at this place. Are you looking?

QUANG. Of course I am.

NHAN. It's beautiful, dude.

QUANG. It's just the desert.

NHAN. It's heaven.

QUANG. It's okay.

NHAN. I thought deserts were just sand and shit, but this is goddamn gorgeous, man.
Look at that sky. I ain't never seen a sky like that. It's like God painted it himself.
With his dick.

QUANG. You're a poet.

NHAN. Pull over.

QUANG. What?

NHAN. Just pull over, man!

> (**QUANG** *does.*)
>
> (**NHAN** *runs out and collapses on his back.*)
>
> (*Silence.*)

QUANG. What are you doing?

NHAN. Shut up. I'm having a moment.

> (**NHAN** *pulls out a joint.*)
>
> (**QUANG** *takes it and lights it for himself.*)
>
> (*They sit in silence a little more.*)

Look, man, there's something I should say to you –
I'm just thinking…maybe we're exactly where we're supposed to be.

QUANG. Bullshit.

NHAN. Well, it ain't all bad here, right? Like there's some good shit here in America, right? Like burritos.

QUANG. Yeah, burritos are pretty good.

NHAN. Like weed.

Like not getting shot at all the time. That's good!

QUANG. That's certainly better for our health.

NHAN. Like...that girl Tong.

QUANG. Who?

NHAN. Don't play dumb, motherfucker. You know who I'm talking about. You were mad into that girl.

QUANG. Yes, I of course remember Tong.

But no, correction, I was not "mad into that girl."

NHAN. Bullshit.

QUANG. I mean, yeah, we hung out and all. But, like, no strings attached or whatever. It was what it was and that was a whole bunch of NOTHING.

NHAN. Okay, then what about –

QUANG. I mean, yeah, sure, she was cool though.

And hot.

Like real hot.

And she made me laugh.

And, damn, she had one nice-ass laugh herself.

You know, the kinda laugh that when you hear it, it makes you wanna laugh too. Like it made bad days seem good.

It was one badass laugh.

NHAN. Yeah, you weren't into that girl at all.

QUANG. Fuck off.

NHAN. So, see, this place ain't that bad, right?

QUANG. Yeah, it is.

NHAN. What? But we just established –

QUANG. 'Cause this place doesn't have my kids, man. It ain't about burritos or safety or even a girl...all that shit is just camouflage, but as much camo as you can put on it, it still doesn't hide the fact that all it's covering up is one big ol' hole that should be occupied by two little kids that look like me. So, yeah, it is "that bad." 'Cause here…I may be alive, but I'm not truly living because here I'll never be a dad.

NHAN. Damn, man.

QUANG. I'll be honest, bro. I have no idea if this plan will really work. For all we know, the Americans will shoot us on sight if we tell them we wanna go back, but I know I'm supposed to be trying to get there. I'm supposed to be a dad. That's what I'm supposed to be doing.

NHAN. Right. My bad.

QUANG. Is that all you wanted to tell me?

NHAN. No. It was… Well, I wanted to tell you…you're my best friend. I love you, man.

QUANG. I knew it. Every time you get fucked up it's always "I love you, man."

NHAN. Don't make fun of me.

QUANG. Hey. I love you too, bro. I do.
     High five.

> *(They high five and hug.)*
>
> *(Cut to…)*
>
> *(A short sequence where **BOBBY** runs into **HUONG**. He's holding a flower for **TONG**, but her mother won't let him pass. He tries a couple of different ways to get passed her, but there's nothing working. Finally, she takes the single flower out of his hand and disposes of it [perhaps by eating it].)*
>
> *(Cut to…)*
>
> *(**QUANG, NHAN**, and **TONG** are eating together.)*
>
> *(**NHAN** sits in between, glaring at them.)*

NHAN. So let me get this right. You two just "do it" and that's all?

QUANG. If by "it," you mean sex. Yes, we just do "it."

TONG. In my vagina.

NHAN. Man, I hate you.

QUANG. What? Why?

NHAN. She's hot.

    You're hot.

    I never get to have sex with hot women.

QUANG. You get laid all the time.

NHAN. Yes, but not with anyone that looks like her.

TONG. "Her" is sitting right here, you know? You can address "her" directly.

NHAN. You're beautiful.

TONG. Thanks. If it makes you feel any better, my personality is absolutely dreadful. I hate everything. EVERYTHING. That includes babies.

NHAN. You hate babies?

TONG. I hate babies. They freak me out. I'm like the sheer opposite of every Vietnamese woman on the planet. I'm anti-maternal.

NHAN. Man, I want a hot woman that hates babies.

TONG. I mean… I love babies?

NHAN. You guys are mocking me.

QUANG. No, we're not.

TONG. Maybe a little.

NHAN. Fuck you guys. I'm out of here. I'm going to go jack off.

        (NHAN leaves.)

QUANG. You know he's going to be picturing you when he does it.

TONG. I'd be offended if he didn't.

        (The two share a laugh.)

QUANG. I like you.

TONG. What?

QUANG. I like you.

TONG. What? No. Don't do that.

QUANG. Don't do what?

TONG. Feel.

QUANG. I can't help having feelings.

TONG. Yes, you can. Look at me. I'm the queen of not feeling shit.

QUANG. Hey, I'm not saying I want to marry you or anything, I'm just saying I think you're alright. Like you're not as much of a bitch as you think you are. Like I like you...as a friend.

TONG. That's it?

QUANG. Yes. That's it.

TONG. Good. Because there's something I should tell you.

QUANG. What's that?

TONG. I'm making love to two other guys as well. Thought you should know.

QUANG. What? WHO? WHO?!

TONG. I thought you didn't care. I thought you only like me as a friend.

QUANG. I don't care. I mean – I guess I do – for STD reasons. I don't want an STD.

TONG. Is that right?

QUANG. Totally. I don't want crabs.

TONG. They're clean. We're safe. No worries. No need to think about them again.
We're cool, right?

QUANG. Right.

TONG. Cool.

QUANG. So...do I know either of them?

TONG. Fuck...

QUANG. What?

TONG. You can't have feelings for me, Quang.

QUANG. I don't. I just – I just need to know about these other guys.

TONG. Why? What difference does it make?

QUANG. It just does, okay? Who are they?

TONG. They're no one. There are no other guys, jackass. I was just proving a point.

QUANG. And what's that?

TONG. Do not fall for me.

QUANG. I'm not –

But even if I were, why is that so bad?

TONG. You're married for one.

QUANG. Besides me being married.

TONG. Because I'm not going to fall for you back. Because I don't believe in that shit. Because love is bullshit.

QUANG. That's crazy.

TONG. It's not crazy.

QUANG. What's the point in life if you don't get to have love in it.

TONG. You know what I "get"? I get a new lease on life. That's what I get. Because, unlike my brother, I was able to escape Vietnam easily because I had no problem leaving behind the guy who was "in love with me."

QUANG. But you lost your home.

TONG. Home was living in a leaf hut – home was a place where I had to lie about my age when I was ten to be able to attend first grade because my parents didn't think girls needed school – home is where all I get to be is pretty, but not heard. Fuck that. Clearly America isn't turning out to be like its travel brochure, but it offers me something Vietnam didn't – it offers me the chance to be me. Viet men all think women are something to be taken care of – a princess to be saved. Look at you, that's exactly what you're wanting/needing to do right now – to save me – to save your wife – to save someone. The thing is I'm no princess and you're no Prince Charming…but I like that about us. I like that I'm not in a fairy tale, but instead writing my own. I like that we can do this without the bullshit veneer of "love" over it. You're a good guy, Quang Nguyen. But you're not "the guy" for me. Because honestly there's no such thing.

QUANG. I think you're wrong.

I hope I'm there to see it when it happens.

TONG. You're going to be waiting for a very long time.

QUANG. It's not like I have anything else better to do.

TONG. I can think of something.

(She gives him a smile.)

QUANG. Really? I'm still in the middle of my lunch –

(TONG knocks the food out of his hand.)

Guess I'm done.

(They take off kissing.)

6.

[Projection: Flagstaff, Arizona]

(**NHAN** *is refueling the bike as the* **REDNECK BIKER** *rides up next to him.*)

REDNECK BIKER. HEY!

NHAN. Oh fuck.

REDNECK BIKER. Ain't y'all – yeehaw – the gook bitches – yeehaw – that knocked me of my bike – yeehaw?

NHAN. Us? No. I've never seen you before in my life. I'm just another fellow motorbiker like yourself.

REDNECK BIKER. You – yeehaw – fucked up my bike – yeehaw.

NHAN. Can I give you money?

REDNECK BIKER. No – yeehaw – but you can lick the bottom of my boot – yeehaw!

> (*The* **REDNECK BIKER** *punches* **NHAN** *in the face.* **NHAN** *tries to fight back, but the* **REDNECK BIKER** *is tough as a motherfucker.*)
>
> (*He starts beating* **NHAN** *down.*)
>
> (**QUANG** *approaches with food in his hand.*)

QUANG. What in the hell?

REDNECK BIKER. Hey – yeehaw – it's your girlfriend – yeehaw.

QUANG. Get away from him now.

> (**QUANG** *steps to the* **REDNECK BIKER.**)
>
> (*As the* **REDNECK BIKER** *goes to throw a punch at* **QUANG**, *everything suddenly freezes.*)

REDNECK BIKER/THE PLAYWRIGHT. According to the real life accounts of Quang Nguyen, this is exactly how this fight went down.

> (*Unfreeze: The* **REDNECK BIKER** *swings a punch at* **QUANG**, *but* **QUANG** *does an elaborate capoeira-esque cartwheel to avoid it.*)

(Badass music begins playing.)

(And suddenly, in the most badass martial arts fight ever to be seen on a theatrical stage, QUANG and the REDNECK BIKER go full-on kung fu madness on each other.)

(QUANG finally lands a substantial blow on the REDNECK BIKER, and he falls down.)

REDNECK BIKER. Back-up – yee-haw! HELP!

(Suddenly, in the middle of the fight, NINJAS appear.)

(Freeze.)

REDNECK BIKER/THE PLAYWRIGHT. Yep, that's right. His backup were ninjas. True story!

(Unfreeze.)

(There are a lot of fancy moves, punches, and kicks thrown by the NINJAS. But in the end, QUANG defeats the NINJAS.)

(The REDNECK BIKER goes for a final attack, but together QUANG and NHAN throw a simultaneous superpunch [performed in slo-mo or bullet-time] that crushes the REDNECK BIKER's face.)

(He falls to the ground.)

QUANG. Let's get the hell out of here. Arizona blows.

(QUANG and NHAN exit like badasses.)

(Cut to…)

(Lights come up on HUONG in front of a make-shift Buddhist temple.)

(She lights a piece of incense and put it in a holder.)

(She bows three times and begins praying out loud.)

HUONG. Please protect my baby boy Khue. Please protect him.

Please protect my baby boy Khue. Please protect him.

Please protect my baby boy –

> *[Projection: Two Months Earlier]*

> *[Projection: Saigon, Vietnam]*

> (KHUE *enters.*)

KHUE. Mom, what are you still doing here?

HUONG. I'm praying.

KHUE. You're supposed to be on a bus to the airport.

HUONG. I'm not going with Tong. I don't do planes.

KHUE. What?

HUONG. Besides she should bring her fiancé to America.

KHUE. Giai?

HUONG. Yes.

KHUE. She doesn't even like Giai.

HUONG. They're engaged. Of course she likes him.

KHUE. What? They're not engaged. She told him no.

HUONG. That's not what she told me –

KHUE. Because she lied to you. That's what she does to
    keep you off her back. She lies.

HUONG. She would never.

KHUE. Yes, she would.

    You're really hard on her.

    She does it so you won't constantly yell at her.

HUONG. I don't yell! I'm making her strong.

KHUE. She could use some soft every now and again.

HUONG. She's my last daughter. She doesn't need to be
    soft. Look what it did for Loc.

    I don't want her to end up like Loc.

KHUE. Loc didn't die because she was soft. She died
    because she got sick.

HUONG. It doesn't matter, I'm staying here to take care of
    you. You're my baby boy.

KHUE. No, Mom, you're going. Get your ass up! Come on.
    COME ON!

HUONG. Why are you getting so worked up? She's just going on vacation.

KHUE. You think she's just going on vacation?

Are you crazy?

Do you not see what's happening at the embassy?

People are swarming it.

HUONG. So?

KHUE. So it's not a vacation. She's escaping.

HUONG. She's leaving?

KHUE. That's why you gotta go, Mom. If you don't, she'll be alone over there.

HUONG. No. Then you should go.

KHUE. I'm not going anywhere without Pham. I told her that. And we all agreed that you're the one that deserves this. You've had a hard life. You lost two husbands, three children, and your own home. We're not going to let you die here as well.

HUONG. What kind of mother would I be if I left my son behind?

KHUE. What kind of brother would I be if I let my sister go to America alone without her mother?

Listen to me – I'm young, I have Pham, I have no connections to the South Vietnamese military, I'll be fine. But my big sister needs you. She may never say it, she may act like a total ass all the time, but down deep, she needs her mommy. You have to go.

HUONG. But what about you?

KHUE. If you love me, trust me. Go.

> *(Lights shift and we're back in Fort Chaffee where* **TONG** *is practicing her spelling on a chalkboard.)*
>
> *(***HUONG*** grabs one of her sandals and throws it at the chalkboard. It startles* **TONG**.*)*

TONG. Shit! You startled me. Don't do that.

HUONG. I'm not going to go.

TONG. What?

HUONG. I'm not going to go.

TONG. Where?

HUONG. Back to Vietnam. I'm going to stay here with you.

TONG. Yeah?

HUONG. Yes.

TONG. Cool. Wanna learn some English?

HUONG. Fuck no.

TONG. Awesome.

> (TONG *continues to spell as* HUONG *watches.*)

HUONG. Tong. One more thing.

TONG. What?

> (HUONG *hugs her.* TONG *is weirded out at first,*
> *but as she notices her mother not letting go, she*
> *finally settles in and hugs her back.*)

HUONG. I love you. I'm here because I love you.

TONG. I love you too, Mommy.

> (*They hold tight onto one another.*)
>
> (*Cut to…*)
>
> (QUANG *working on a motorcycle.*)
>
> (TONG *enters.*)

Hey.

QUANG. Hey!

TONG. When did you get this?

QUANG. Found it.

TONG. You found it?

QUANG. Yeah, it's an old bike that was in a storage shed. Talked to the folks here and they said I could have it. So I'm fixing it up. Isn't she beautiful?

TONG. Do you usually look at excrement and find it appealing? Because this is a piece of shit.

QUANG. Don't listen to the crazy lady, baby. We got this.

TONG. Are you serious with the whole talking to the bike thing?

QUANG. No.

    (Yes.)

TONG. Cute.

QUANG. What's up your ass?

TONG. What?

QUANG. You got a look. What's up with that?

TONG. It's not a look. It's my face.

QUANG. Well, your face has a look that's making it look kinda…mopey.

TONG. It's not mopey. It's sort of confused-slash-wierded out. My mom just hugged me.

QUANG. Aw.

TONG. No, not aw. "Aw" would be if she hugged me all the time and this was just another moment of regular mother/daughter affection for her. But it's not. It was out of the ordinary.

QUANG. Or she's been here long enough to know that when it comes to those we love, time is precious.

TONG. That doesn't sound like her.

QUANG. Why are you so surprised? She's your mom. If I were her, I'd want to hug you all the time.

TONG. You would, would you?

QUANG. I would. Seriously. Truth is if it weren't for you, I'd just be moping around this place all the time. But I don't because you make this place seem pretty alright.

TONG. Ah, because of the sex –

QUANG. No, dummy. Because of you. You're awesome. You make me…well, you make me want to wake up every morning just to be able to hang out with you.

TONG. Oh.

QUANG. Sorry. That sounded less cheesy in my head than it did out loud.

TONG. No, it's cool.

    (Beat.)

You should bring me out to dinner.

QUANG. In the cafeteria?

TONG. No. Like out. Like to a restaurant.

QUANG. Why would I do that?

TONG. Well...

QUANG. Oh. But I thought you didn't believe in –

TONG. I know.

I just thought –

You're here, I'm here – it might be fun.

There's a diner maybe a mile down the road that I like sneaking off to. We could take your bike.

QUANG. My bike. Right.

TONG. They make grilled cheese sandwiches. I love grilled cheese sandwiches.

But there's other stuff on their menu that I can't read and your English is better than mine so I thought –

QUANG. I can't.

TONG. What?

QUANG. I can't.

That's why I have this bike.

I'm gonna use it to drive to California.

TONG. When?

QUANG. Soon.

There's a plane that's flying from Camp Pendleton to Guam.

Nhan and I are gonna go catch it.

TONG. Oh.

QUANG. I'm sorry.

TONG. It's cool. I don't give a shit. Whatever. You're going back to Vietnam. Whatever. It's your life. I'm not part of it. You do what you need to do.

QUANG. Hey.

TONG. I was going to tell you that I got my foster family assignment. In some small town called El Dorado, Arkansas. I can't wait. Maybe I'll make some friends there that aren't going to bail on me.

QUANG. Tong.

TONG. Have fun on your bike ride.

Seriously.

It was awesome meeting you.

Drive safe.

> (**TONG** *walks away.*)
>
> (*As she does…*)
>
> (*A beat drops.*)
>
> **[Music Cue 06: "I Don't Give a Shit"]**

LOVE IS JUST SOME BULLSHIT STORY
A POETIC VENEER ON WHY WE GET HORNY
BUT I DON'T NEED YOUR FLOWERS OR YOUR LOVE
SHOUT-OUTS
JUST GIMME WHAT I NEED AND GET THE FUCK ON OUT

OH – CALL ME A WHORE AS I KICK YOU OUT THE DOOR
BUT LEMME BE CLEAR – YO, THIS IS THE SCORE
I JUST NEEDED YOUR DICK TO SCRATCH A LITTLE ITCH
IF YOU WANNA FALL IN LOVE, GO FIND SOME OTHER BITCH

I DON'T GIVE A DAMN IF I'M IN YOUR DIARY
I'M NO JULIET WAITING ON NO BALCONY
WANNA BE A ROMEO, THEN YOU SHOULD KNOW 'BOUT ME
NOT GONNA DRINK NO POISON, WON'T STAB MYSELF FOR
THEE

I DON'T NEED NO ROSES OR TO CALL YOU MINE
'CAUSE DECREEING YOUR LOVE IS JUST A WASTE OF TIME
I'M NOT SOME LITTLE GIRL DREAMING FOR HER PRINCE
I CAN SAVE MY OWN KINGDOM, I'M A BADASS BITCH

SO – KEEP YOUR CARDS AND YOUR HEART-SHAPED CANDIES
THAT SHIT IS STUPID – SAVE YOUR MONEY
FUCK A BUNCH OF LOVE, LIFE IS TOO SHORT
WHO WANTS ONLY ONE WHEN YOU CAN HAVE SO MUCH
MORE

IMMA KEEP RUNNING TILL I GET ME MINE
DON'T NEED YOUR LOVE, ROLLING SOLO'S FINE

IF LOSING MY BROTHER CAN'T MESS ME UP
MY HEART'S ROCK HARD NOW, I DON'T GIVE A FUCK

MY SKIN'S NOW TOUGH LIKE RHINO HIDE
HIT ME HARD, THESE EYES DON'T CRY
KNOCK ME OVER, I JUST STAND RIGHT UP
AND THEN I'LL LAUGH IN YOUR FACE BEFORE I FUCK YOU
UP

YOU THINK I GIVE A DAMN THAT YOU LEFT ME HERE?
WE'RE NOT IN CAMELOT, I'M NO GUINEVERE
YO, A DICK IS JUST A DICK, A KNIGHT IS JUST A KNIGHT
FUCK YOU, LANCELOT, I CAN FIGHT MY OWN FIGHTS

I DON'T GIVE A SHIT, I DON'T GIVE A SHIT, GIVE A SHIT
I DON'T GIVE A SHIT, I DON'T GIVE A SHIT, GIVE A SHIT
I DON'T GIVE A SHIT, I DON'T GIVE A SHIT, GIVE A SHIT
I DON'T GIVE A SHIT, I DON'T GIVE A SHIT, GIVE A SHIT

I DON'T GIVE A SHIT, I DON'T GIVE A SHIT, GIVE A SHIT
I DON'T GIVE A SHIT, I DON'T GIVE A SHIT, GIVE A SHIT
I DON'T GIVE A SHIT, I DON'T GIVE A SHIT, GIVE A SHIT
I DON'T GIVE A...

(Cut to...)

[Projection: Diner Outside of Fort Chaffee]

(Lights up on TONG *and* BOBBY.*)*

BOBBY. Thanks you for having dinner with me.

TONG. Thank you for asking. So what are we having?

BOBBY. Steak hamburger.

TONG. Oh. A plate of meat. Great. It looks...good.

BOBBY. Yum yum.

TONG. Your Vietnamese is getting better.

BOBBY. Botanical.

TONG. What?

BOBBY. Barometer.

TONG. Maybe I spoke too soon.

BOBBY. No. Trying to find right word. I find you very...
beautiful tonight.

TONG. Thank you.

BOBBY. Seeing you for original time was love in eyeball
originals.

TONG. What?

BOBBY. No. That's all wrong.
Frickles!

TONG. Say it slow.

BOBBY. Okay.
Like you I.

TONG. Oh.

BOBBY. No.
I like you.

TONG. I know.

BOBBY. Seeing you for first time was love in sight first.

TONG. Oh.

BOBBY. I sorry. I'm sorry. Maybe I telling too fast.

TONG. No, it's okay. It's fine.

BOBBY. Yeah.

TONG. I like you too.

BOBBY. Yes?

TONG. Yes.

> *(They kiss as* **QUANG** *enters the restaurant with
> flowers in hand.)*
>
> *(He sees them share a moment together and tosses
> the flowers in the trash.)*

7.

[Projection: Oceanside, California]

QUANG. Do you smell that? Do you smell it?

NHAN. What? Did you fart or something?

QUANG. No, ass-for-brains. I'm talking about the ocean.

NHAN. Yeah, it smells like the ocean.

QUANG. It smells like home.

It's the Pacific. Same body of water that Vietnam's in. Same ocean that touches our home.

NHAN. You're stoned right now, aren't you?

QUANG. No, I'm having a moment.

NHAN. Can you be done with your moment already?

I really gotta piss.

QUANG. We made it. Why aren't you happy about this? This is why we've been on a fucking motorcycle for a week. So we can be here – so we can go home.

NHAN. That's not why we've been on the road for five days. That's why you've been on the road, but not "we." We aren't on the same page about our travel objectives.

QUANG. Bullshit. You said you wanted to come.

NHAN. I know.

But not to Vietnam.

QUANG. You just wanted to ride bitch on my bike for fun?

NHAN. No, dummy, I've been riding with you to convince you to stop.

QUANG. Stop?

NHAN. Stop with this crazy ass plan of yours, man. There's no home to go home to.

QUANG. Fuck you.

NHAN. Homie, you are my bro. We've been through the shit – the real shit together – and as your bro, I'm telling you straight up – this plan of yours is fucking dumbass as hell.

QUANG. I will kick your ass.

NHAN. Then kick my ass. But don't go.

QUANG. There's nothing for us here.

NHAN. There's even less there.

QUANG. Bullshit.

NHAN. Man, what do you think is gonna happen exactly? You think you're gonna step off that ship and do what? Just go home? Be with your family? You were the captain of a ten helicopter squadron, a military officer in the Republic of Vietnam's Air Force that trained here in America. Do you know what happens to that guy when he steps into Vietnam?

Do you?

What happens to that guy?

QUANG. I don't –

NHAN. He DIES.

At best that is. At best they put a goddamn bullet in your brain as soon as they see you because the other option – the other option is they put you in one of their camps. And we're not talking some cushy two-year re-education cake walk, we're talking the rest of your goddamn life.

QUANG. You're not telling anything I don't already know. I'll be fine.

NHAN. What good are you going to do for your wife, for your kids, for anyone if you're dead or locked up?

QUANG. At least I'll be near them.

NHAN. You'll be a ghost.

QUANG. Yeah, but a ghost who did everything he could to get home – to be with his family.

NHAN. No, man. That's what you'll be to you. To you, if you go back, whether you die or get locked up, the only person here who gets anything out of your "heroic act" is you. You get to feel like a hero, but for them, all you will be is a reminder that they're not allowed to move on. That for the rest of their lives, all they can do is live in the shadow of their suffering husband and father. Your sorrow will be their reality. Is that what you want for them?

QUANG. ...

NHAN. If you love them, if you really fucking love them – the best thing you can do is let them go.

QUANG. But they're my family –

NHAN. I know.

But this is what you gotta understand, man.

You're dead.

We all are.

We died the moment the VC crossed Newport Bridge into Saigon and you flew us the fuck outta there to save us. And that's what you did, you saved a lot of lives that day, but there was one life that got lost and that was yours. Let Thu and your kids mourn you. Let them say their goodbyes. And then let them find some new happiness because it's not going to be with you. Bottom line, brotha – let them go.

QUANG. So all this was for nothing? Everything we just went through, it's all worth shit?

NHAN. Yeah, man.

That's what happens during war.

(QUANG *looks over at his motorcycle.*)

(*He takes his helmet or backpack [whatever's handy] and starts violently smashing it into his bike as he screams in futility at it.*)

QUANG. *(Yells.)* Aaagh!

(*Cut to...*)

[Projection: Three Months Later]

[Projection: El Dorado, Arkansas]

(*Lights up on* BOBBY *standing on a front porch. He paces nervously.*)

(TONG *and* HUONG *are returning home with groceries.*)

BOBBY. Hi! Hello, pretty girl.

Hello, old lady! It is good to greet you here.

TONG. Hey Bobby.

HUONG. Hey dumbass.

BOBBY. Help you can I with big bag?

HUONG. No.

BOBBY. Help me let you.

HUONG. If you don't let go of my bags, I will stab you, dumbass!

BOBBY. You are very sweet old lady, old lady, but let me –

HUONG. NO!

> (**HUONG** *pulls her bags away and goes into the house.*)

BOBBY. Your mother warming to me, yes?

HUONG. *(Offstage.)* Tell him to go the fuck home!

BOBBY. I flower for you.

TONG. You know you don't always have to get me flowers, right?

BOBBY. I sorry.

TONG. You don't have to apologize.

BOBBY. I here wanting ask big question.

TONG. What?

BOBBY. Tong Thi Tran –

TONG. Oh god…

BOBBY. Will you go to dinner date with me?

TONG. Dinner?

BOBBY. Yes.

TONG. Dinner? Like to a restaurant?

BOBBY. Yes.

TONG. That's it?

BOBBY. It very special restaurant. Friend of mine call Paul Dairy Diner make special table for us. And there I have thing – very super special thing – that I wanting to giving you.

TONG. Oh.

BOBBY. You happy making me very much.
   Will you come?

TONG. Uh, sure, I guess.

BOBBY. Celebrations!

> (**HUONG** *returns.*)

HUONG. Seriously, are you going to help me with the groceries or not?

TONG. I should go.

BOBBY. I picking you up here tonight at eight o'clock?

TONG. I'll be right here.

BOBBY. Can I kissing you?

TONG. Of course, you can. You don't always have to ask.

> (**BOBBY** *leans in to kiss* **TONG**.)

HUONG. Wow. This is so romantic.

TONG. Shut up, Mom.

BOBBY. I'll be back tonight. You love princess awesome happy!

> (**BOBBY** *leaves.*)

HUONG. Seriously, this is who you want stuffing your spring roll?

TONG. Don't be gross.

HUONG. What's wrong with you?

TONG. Nothing. I just have some things to think about.

HUONG. Like what?

TONG. Like nothing that you would care about. Let's just go put away our stuff.

HUONG. Hey. Wait just a minute.
   Can I talk to you?

TONG. About what, Mom?

HUONG. You don't have to settle.

TONG. What?

HUONG. I see you with him.
   There's no fire.

TONG. Fire? Really? Are you really telling me this? You, the woman who makes comments on the daily about my empty womb, are really worried about "fire"?

HUONG. Just because I think you'd be happy having a child – or three – doesn't mean I want you to have one with just anyone. Especially with just some dumbass.

TONG. He's a good guy.

HUONG. He's a dumb guy.

TONG. He's not dumb.

HUONG. "You love princess awesome happy!"

TONG. So his Vietnamese sucks, have you heard your sad attempts at English.

HUONG. English is also dumb.

TONG. I like him.

HUONG. Do you?

TONG. I do. He's nice. He's loyal. He sticks around and he'll do absolutely anything to make sure I'm happy.

HUONG. But do you love him?

TONG. Yes. I love him. I love him so much. He makes me see rainbows.

HUONG. Bullshit.

TONG. Why does that even matter?

HUONG. Because it's the only thing that matters when it comes to being with someone.

TONG. Oh god, please, you sound just like –

HUONG. Like who?

TONG. No one. Let's just go inside.

HUONG. Tong, listen to me. I know you think that this makes you strong – that putting up these walls will keep you from ever being hurt, but look at me. Do you think I'm weak? I lived through what you lived through – I'm also strong – but I also know love. I've known love from two amazing men and one of them gave me one amazing daughter who's a survivor, a warrior, and a woman who saved me from a war…but that doesn't mean she has to keep fighting on her own alone. Love doesn't make you weak, it's what gives us strength during the fight.

TONG. Well then I'm tired of fighting.

HUONG. Then let me help you.

Hey DUMMY, that's your cue.

TONG. What?

(QUANG *approaches.*)

QUANG. What's up, hot stuff?

TONG. Quang?

HUONG. Actually, I think I can put away the groceries myself.

(HUONG *exits.*)

TONG. What are you doing here?

QUANG. I came here to see you obviously.

TONG. How?

QUANG. Your mom.

TONG. My mom?

QUANG. She's my pen pal.

TONG. Where the hell have you been?

QUANG. Camp Pendleton, California then went up to San Jose for a bit to make money. Turns out that plane tickets are mad expensive.

TONG. So you just came here to –

QUANG. To take you out to dinner.

TONG. I already have dinner plans.

QUANG. Then lunch.

TONG. I'm with someone –

QUANG. You mean that white guy who speaks like a broken robot?

TONG. He's sweet.

QUANG. He's wrong for you.

TONG. This coming from the married guy who took off the moment it got slightly real between us.

QUANG. I wasn't running away from you. I was running to… Well, to nothing as it turns out.

TONG. I don't know what you or my mom's thinking, but I'm not going to be your consolation prize. You're married. I get that. Doing what we were doing was –

QUANG. Shut up.

I care about you.

TONG. Great.

QUANG. No. Listen.

I care about you, dummy.

And I'm not here asking you to marry me or run off with me or even to fall in love with me. I just… You're the only thing in this country – maybe even in this world – that even makes a lick of sense to me.

You and I speak the same language.

TONG. There's other Vietnamese girls here, Quang.

QUANG. That's not the language I'm referring to.

You and I understand each other.

TONG. I'm a mess.

QUANG. Have you not seen me?

TONG. I care about you too, it's just –

QUANG. Then let's go get some food. We'll have drinks, we'll have some laughs.

TONG. I have a boyfriend.

QUANG. That's cool. I have a wife.

TONG. He's going to propose to me tonight.

QUANG. Well then I guess I have five hours to give you a reason to say no.

What do you say?

TONG. I'm not going to sleep with you.

QUANG. Hey! No spoilers.

TONG. I'm not even going to kiss you.

QUANG. Okay.

TONG. And I'm definitely not going to fall for you if that's what you're hoping.

QUANG. So is that a yes?

TONG. Fine. One drink. That's it.

QUANG. Cool.

One more thing...

TONG. What's that?

> (QUANG *grabs her and kisses her.*)
>
> (*She tries to fight it, but quickly succumbs and kisses him back, hard.*)

Hey. I told you I wasn't going to kiss you.

QUANG. I didn't say I wasn't going to kiss you though.

TONG. You're a fucking asshole.

QUANG. No arguments here.

> (*She grabs him and kisses him more.*)
>
> (*Music begins to play.*)
>
> (*In the background, we see the dates tick forward from 1976 to the present as the* **PLAYWRIGHT** *enters and assists* **TONG** *and* **QUANG**'s *transformation from young lovers to his older parents.*)

Epilogue

[Projection: 2015]

(Focus on a present-day **QUANG** *and his son* *[***PLAYWRIGHT***]. They are sitting across from one another at a dinner table.)*

(There's beers stacked on **QUANG***'s side of the table.)*

*(***PLAYWRIGHT** *wears headphones and fumbles with a mic and computer.)*

(For the first time in the play, **QUANG** *now speaks with a deep Vietnamese accent.)*

PLAYWRIGHT. Dad. Dad, you ready?

Okay, say something into the mic.

QUANG.

  MAMA, DON'T LET YOU BABY / GROW UP TO BE COWBOY!
Sing with me!

PLAYWRIGHT. Dad, can you please just try to focus. Just a little?

QUANG. Ooo! You know who should play me?

PLAYWRIGHT. Who?

QUANG. Harrison Ford.

PLAYWRIGHT. You want Indiana Jones to play you?

QUANG. He good actor.

PLAYWRIGHT. He's white.

QUANG. I knowing he is white.

PLAYWRIGHT. And you're Asian.

QUANG. Son, I telling you secret. White people love playing Oriental. Mickey Rooney. Yul Brynner. David Carradine. They all wanting to be Oriental. Just like you and me.

PLAYWRIGHT. I don't think that's what it is.

QUANG. IT IS!

PLAYWRIGHT. And, by the way, we go by "Asians" now, not "Orientals" –

QUANG. Same thing.

PLAYWRIGHT. It's not the same thing.

Okay, I think I got this working now.

You ready?

Date: August 7, 2015.

Interview with Quang Nguyen.

Okay, Dad, what can you tell me about Vietnam?

QUANG. You know first time I ever changing your diaper, you poop in my hand.

PLAYWRIGHT. What?

QUANG. I have no idea what to do, so a put hand under butt

to / catch your poo-poo –

PLAYWRIGHT. Dad, that has nothing to do with Vietnam –

QUANG. But then you start peeing and I use / other hand to block it –

PLAYWRIGHT. Can you stop?

QUANG. So it spray onto my hand and I go –

"Oh no, what do I do? / This so crazy!"

PLAYWRIGHT. You're just going to keep talking, aren't you?

QUANG. And then I put my hand on head like this. And it had poop in it. And it got all over me. It so stinky!

PLAYWRIGHT. Are you finished?

QUANG. You should put that story in play.

PLAYWRIGHT. No, I'm not going to put a story about me pooping in your hand into my play.

QUANG. I think it be good story to tell.

PLAYWRIGHT. Dad, are you drunk?

QUANG. I just want to be loose. My son wanting to write a play about me! I so proud! I wanting us to have good time! Now you sing with me!

PLAYWRIGHT. No.

QUANG. I knowing you know the words. I sing it to you all time when you baby.

    DON'T LET THEM PICK GUITAR / OR DRIVE A OLD TRUCK!

PLAYWRIGHT. No, Dad! NO!

QUANG. Why you so serious?

PLAYWRIGHT. Because, Dad, I'm trying to do something important here.

    Something about you, about Mom, about Vietnam.

QUANG. Did you interview your mommy already?

PLAYWRIGHT. Yes.

QUANG. What she tell you?

PLAYWRIGHT. A lot – I don't know – stuff – but I need your perspective –

QUANG. Did she tell you about Giai?

PLAYWRIGHT. Giai? Who's Giai?

QUANG. Did she not bring him up?

PLAYWRIGHT. Dad, we talked for five hours. I have no idea. I haven't gone through all my notes – Is he a relative?

QUANG. No.

PLAYWRIGHT. Then who is he?

QUANG. I don't know.

PLAYWRIGHT. What do you mean you don't know? You just asked me about him.

QUANG. Maybe he's important – maybe not.

PLAYWRIGHT. The fuck, Dad? What are you talking about?

QUANG. Okay, you not say anything to Mommy about this, but Giai…he was your mother's old boyfriend. They were to be married, I think. But Saigon fell and she escaped. He did not. I think maybe she still love him.

PLAYWRIGHT. Holy shit.

QUANG. I know. Very shocking.

PLAYWRIGHT. Holy fucking shit, Dad, are you serious?

QUANG. I am.

PLAYWRIGHT. You've been married to Mom for forty years and you're still sweating her high school boyfriend?

What are you, sixty-three going on sixteen? Jesus Christ, Dad!

QUANG. So she not bring up Giai?

PLAYWRIGHT. NO! Why would she?

QUANG. Okay, then no big deal…

PLAYWRIGHT. Dad, I want to know about Vietnam!

Not Mom's ex-boyfriends!

VIETNAM! TELL ME ABOUT VIETNAM! What were you doing in Vietnam in 1968?

QUANG. Nothing.

PLAYWRIGHT. Nothing?

QUANG. Nothing.

PLAYWRIGHT. But you were in the military.

QUANG. Yes.

PLAYWRIGHT. The Air Force.

QUANG. Yes.

PLAYWRIGHT. So how could you have been doing nothing in Vietnam in 1968?

QUANG. Because I was not in Vietnam in 1968.

I was here. In America.

PLAYWRIGHT. Wait, you came here in 1975.

QUANG. That true. When I escape. But before Saigon fall, I come here in 1968 for one and a half year.

PLAYWRIGHT. I didn't know that.

QUANG. Surprise. There many thing you don't know.

PLAYWRIGHT. What were you doing here?

QUANG. How you think I learn to fly helicopter?

PLAYWRIGHT. The Air Force taught you.

QUANG. Yes. The American Air Force.

PLAYWRIGHT. That doesn't make sense –

QUANG. Funny fact, Americans not only ones who fighting for South Vietnam during Vietnam War. South Vietnamese fighting for South Vietnam too.

PLAYWRIGHT. Did you ever fight on the ground?

QUANG. Ha! Remember when I ground you when you thirteen year old for shoplifting in K-Mart?

PLAYWRIGHT. Dad.

QUANG. I not knowing what grounding is so I still letting you go out to movie. I not so good at grounding.

PLAYWRIGHT. Dad, PLEASE! We were getting somewhere.

QUANG. Why you care so much about Vietnam War?

PLAYWRIGHT. Because I want to write something about you.

QUANG. Then let's talk about me grounding you.

PLAYWRIGHT. That's not important.

QUANG. To me, it is.

PLAYWRIGHT. No one cares about how you grounded me or how you couldn't change my diaper. That's boring everyday shit.

QUANG. It my boring everyday shit.

PLAYWRIGHT. Dad –

QUANG. My life is more than the eight years I fight.

PLAYWRIGHT. I know. But it's a big deal –

QUANG. Why?

PLAYWRIGHT. Because it was a war. A really fucked up war.

QUANG. Because we lost.

PLAYWRIGHT. No, because Americans needlessly died in it.

QUANG. How you know this?

PLAYWRIGHT. Jesus, Dad, because it's a foregone conclusion by everyone that Vietnam was one of the biggest military mistakes in all of history. America should have never gotten involved. We had no right to be there.

QUANG. We?

PLAYWRIGHT. Yes. We. America. We had no right –

QUANG. SHUT UP!

PLAYWRIGHT. Dad?

QUANG. You shut up right now. You sound like stupid dummy!

PLAYWRIGHT. Dad.

QUANG. Son, I love you. You very smart, but sometimes when you talk, you sound stupid like shit.

PLAYWRIGHT. …

QUANG. Yes, son, you raised in America and you are American. You work in business with many white people, many black people, many "Asian" people, but – listen to me – you are not white, you are not black, you are not even "Asian." You are Vietnamese. Like me. Like your mother.

And to Vietnamese, the war was not political, it was real. It not something we choose or not choose to be in. The Viet Cong was killing us, stealing what we work so hard to have. They kidnapped our people, murdered, raped, and humiliated our people so they can destroy our spirit, crush our hope, and take away our dignity.

We fight because it was only thing we could do. But we not choose to be in war. War came to us.

And when America come, they gave us hope. They fought beside us as we fought beside them. Yes, there were very many mistakes. A lot bad things happened. But that not change this one fact, many of them died so I could live – so I can be here right now.

When your house is on fire and you lose everything, you do not want to hear from your neighbor that moving into the house was mistake in first place. You especially don't want to hear that the men and women who helped fight that fire were mistakes as well.

When I first come to America, that's all I hear. Very nice, very "smart" young people apologizing for "America's interference." I tell you before "America's interference," we were getting slaughtered. And now, forty years later, all I hear is politicians using Vietnam as a symbol for a mistake. "If the President not careful, this will be another Vietnam." This is not how any Vietnamese wants Vietnam to be remembered.

QUANG. Son, if you wanting to know about Vietnam then I will tell you about Vietnam. If you wanting to know about Vietnamese people, then let me tell you about its people. But if you only wanting to know about war, then go rent a movie.

Stick to writing funny plays, son, this stuff too sad for old man like me to recount just to help you write just another war story.

> (QUANG *opens another beer and quietly drinks it.* PLAYWRIGHT *watches him for a moment and decides to click off the recorder.*)

PLAYWRIGHT.

MAMAS, DON'T LET YOUR BABIES GROW UP TO BE COWBOYS.

> (QUANG *looks at his son.*)

DON'T LET 'EM PICK GUITARS OR DRIVE THEM OLD TRUCKS.

QUANG. *(Joining in.)*

LET 'EM BE DOCTORS AND LAWYERS AND SUCH.

BOTH.

MAMAS DON'T LET YOUR BABIES GROW UP TO BE COWBOYS.
'CAUSE THEY'LL NEVER STAY HOME AND THEY'RE ALWAYS ALONE.
EVEN WITH SOMEONE THEY LOVE.

> (*Lights down.*)

End of Play